It's a Dogs Life – Part 2

DAVE GINNELLY

FOREWORD

ADULT CONTENT

This is another instalment of my life which is quite funny in parts but occasionally my dad also contributes on certain matters to give them a little additional clarity. It is a funny account although throughout the book there are also very serious issues to take into account. Dad highlights these very serious issues but I am confident that you will certainly laugh and smile on many occasions.

The humour is all very tongue in cheek and satirical but hopefully you will realise that and hopefully enjoy the journey with me.

Before any of you venture any too far into the book I feel it is important to recognise any individual who has mental health issues. My dad "silly bollox" has suffered throughout his whole life with very complex issues and the only way to moderate his behaviour is through very strong medication.

He is far from embarrassed about the situation and accepts that is how he will always be. Throughout this book whatever he finds humorous you may not and also whatever he finds serious you may not because his mind is much more complex than your own.

My dad just sees himself as slightly eccentric BUT if you want a second opinion his psychiatrist will tell you he is a danger to himself and also the public. In a nutshell its best we keep him in his shell

AUTHOR HISTORY

Dave Ginnelly Author is a Facebook Page
with links to Amazon.
Stella G. Ginnelly is Stella's Facebook Page.

PREVIOUS BOOKS

Wellies and Warders

Never a Dull Moment

It's a Dogs Life

Bloodlust

ACKNOWLEDGEMENTS

Betty Adams. Jason and Lisa Ashby. Andy
Crampton. Matt Barber. Mick Fox. Caron
Morton. Lee Cass. Janet Duffy.
Charlie Bronson Salvador. Free the artist

SPECIAL MENTIONS

Betty Adams (Proof Reading) Paul Allen. Gia
Amos. David Bishop (artwork and cover)
Janet Duffy (Typing and Editing)

IN MEMORY

Bradd Darby
Paula Salvador

R.I.P. to both of the above. Death is never easy to take but this year more than any other has brought a lot of pain and grief due to the deaths of both of the above people.

CHAPTER ONE

Ahoy shipmates! Who remembers me and my Dad? The bloke I fondly call "Silly Bollox". Not a lot has changed since we wrote our last book apart from we have both aged a little and the years have been kinder to me than they have to him. Yes I've got a few odd signs of age here and there with a few grey whiskers but all in all I'm happy with my appearance.

With "Silly Bollox" his very erratic behaviour, led to the introduction of other new medications linked to the treatment of schizophrenia but I could have told any of the psychiatrists this to be honest. Who better to ask because I live with him on a daily basis? When the diagnosis is to do with a split personality that

6

suggests that there are two people but I can assure every last one of you that this arsehole has got a minimum of TEN people who live in his head! It matters little to me because I love him dearly and will always do so for rescuing me at the time when he did and always giving me the best of everything. The new medication he gets, I have to measure out the doses each day and when I give him his little cup with all his tablets in; it has every colour of the rainbow in the cup.

Overnight, I just seem to have become his Carer or Nurse as he prefers to call me. When he was first prescribed the new medication, I would get the little trampoline out, which is there for when the Grandchildren visit. I would gently bounce on it until I was high enough to jump off on the work surface where the first aid box was. Because it was new to his body and hadn't been accepted yet; it was quite a funny procedure because I would give him the numerous tablets to swallow. Then I would jump

7

up onto the coffee table and stare into his eyes which would be spinning like the reels on a one armed bandit. I would get up on my hind paws and just tap dance backwards and forwards in front of him while juggling with ashtrays but he would see nothing; his eyes would be going boss eyed with the effects.

Some days for fun I would mix the medication up a little and double up on one or not give him one of his important ones and I would take notes of the outcome to have fun on another day. I would need to be very careful though, not to send him too far over the edge. As the memory was still fresh in my head of him chasing two bailiffs with a machete which in normal circumstances is quite extreme BUT to be doing it stark bullock naked takes things to a completely different level I'd say and I'm sure many of the screaming neighbours would agree. To this day I'm not sure if they were screaming at the incident itself or the nudity.

Fortunately "Silly Bollox" is a very likable rogue and gets on with everybody or he would have been dragged away many years before by the men in white suits. Out of all bad comes good and the bailiffs took the wise decision to not come knocking at our door again.

I'm meant to be a guard dog but who needs one of them when you have a six foot naked lunatic with bulging eyes coming towards you. Down the years I have come to understand the signs of what sort of day we were likely to have and for sure if he came downstairs with no clothes on or even semi nude I would realise instantly the day was going to be a very trying one. On these days I would need to drag the trampoline towards the front door, I would bounce up and down a few times, until my teeth made contact with the handle and opened the door. I could then take myself out and down the canal for my own toilet breaks.

9

Around the estate I would bump into many of Dad's friends and they would always ask "how's your Dad Stella"? No way would I ever say that he had got the settee up tight against one of the radiators and he was building one of his "dens"; a secret hiding place, where he could pop his head out the other end. To gather his mail in with a wooden stick, which had a spike on the end to drag the mail towards him? I had a habit of sitting on top of the chair in the bay window when I was bored and look out of the window at the passing traffic or people walking by. If he popped his head out and saw me up there he would praise me and say "good girl Stella, keep your eyes open for them". I would look back at him and think "look out for who you silly twat" but I'd never let him think any different because his head already had him convinced about "The Others".

It wasn't just us pair that lived in the flat I had accepted many years before that I lived in shared accommodation with "The Others" but they would get the blame for most things that went wrong so I was always in the clear and never got reprimanded for nothing. In actual fact I was his nodding dog because anything he thought was amiss in the flat he would say "have you seen what they've done now Stella" and oh I would readily agree and keep myself out of harm's way. These would be isolated incidents to be honest and most days we would have a very peaceful existence with little or no paranoia at all.

I had recently got over a little cancer scare at the PDSA over in Coventry. I think it touched a few nerves with "Silly Bollox" because even though I was now fourteen years of age. He perhaps had never considered the possibility of me ever being ill or even not around at all anymore because sixteen years is the life span of my particular breed and I think it sort of motivated him to start going places.

11

He has recently qualified for his free bus pass to use throughout the UK and we set about using it to go to remote place we hadn't been before. We took in all the sights at Atherstone, Barwell, Coventry, Birmingham, Earl Shilton and other places. We could always be found on the back seat of the buses waving to everyone on the street like Royalty. We would be a very happy little pair on our little adventures like Tom Sawyer and Huckleberry Finn the young boy adventurers.

As is usually the case though, we still found our share of drama. On one visit to Coventry we found somewhere for me to swim and then between me having a dip in the water Dad would have a pint at one of the pubs in the city centre. When we went to leave one pub we discovered the whole area was cordoned off because a young boy had been stabbed in the middle of the afternoon in broad daylight and we chose to strike that area off our list. On another occasion whilst visiting Leicester Dad had never been before except to the football ground so we rode all the way into the bus station so that we knew our way back later on. It was a very hot day but I will admit I can be a bit of a diva and pretended the pavement was a little too hot until it reached the stage that "Silly Bollox" actually carried me in his arms. I winked at many of the people that walked past because I wrap this one round my little finger.

I've seen the latest editions at the coast where the owners push their pets around in a doggy pram and he said "don't even think about it". I could get one if I put my mind to it but I wouldn't want him to lose any of his standing and street cred. A doggy pram would be a bridge too far I reckon ha ha. Anyway I digress; while Dad is carrying me a police constable said there is a fountain around the corner up the next street if you want to cool the dog down and fountains are my speciality because I have been in lots

13

throughout the country. So without further ado I dive out of Dads arms and run and do a skip and a hop and a back flip and hit the water with a very big splash because I like to make a big entrance. The area was quite a big one with lots of people enjoying their lunch breaks. Many of them laughed and cheered at me as I had set about my usual task of bringing all of the empty plastic bottles out of the water and dropping them at Dads feet, I do it anyway at many places I swim but I was now playing to the crowd each time I came out with one. This brought me to the attention of two jobsworths with clip boards, who approached Dad and were quite rude. One of them said "What the fuck do you think you are playing at, does it look like a fucking swimming pool? Get your dog out of there". Oh dear I thought this is not going to end well at all because I know due to brutality against him in his early years he resented any form of authority and I put my paw over my eyes because I couldn't bear to look at the next development. Although, curiosity got the better of me and I sort of flipped over and floated towards them doing a little backstroke, just in time to hear Dad say "the only way my dog is coming out of the water is if you get thrown in and take its place". That was enough to get one of the jobsworths to scurry away to safety and leaving his friend to face the full force of Dads rage which by now had erupted like a volcano.

I watched with interest and I thought well at least Dad has still got his clothes on so his mental instability is still in check but once he blows he is like Doctor David Banner in the Hulk. I sat on the edge of the fountain now because I could see it had gone up a level and I would maybe need to race to the man's rescue. Dad tapped him on the shoulder and informed him that it was a member of the police that had sent him here as he was concerned about his dog's welfare in the scorching heat. "Don't you put your fingers on me" he screamed at Dad and I now feared for the worst because I have seen my Dad before in similar situations. The red rag had been waved at the bull as my Dad grabbed his privates and said to the man "I will make you fucking suck these you halfwit" and there in an instant it had all spiralled out of control and Dad was glaring at everyone in sight with threatening gestures. It is not good for my heart watching it develop all because I had a little swim and recycled the plastic. The man that day, who I supposed worked for the local council does not know how lucky   he was because my "Silly Bollox" is one of the biggest lunatics this country had to offer. I often have to do a role reversal with him; it's me who leads him away on a chain to a quieter area.

We enjoyed the rest of our day and had a fantastic pub crawl and Dad met lots of new faces and got very drunk until his Muslim friend Saimah Vorajee came to pick us both up. She asked Dad how his day had gone and he replied fine because he had already forgot about the earlier incident that could have landed him back in jail.

Oh the joys of living with a serious nut case but the one thing you can be sure of is life will never be dull. I swim in many more fountains and get involved in many more dramas as you will read in later chapters. I'm "Silly Bollox" daughter so you'd expect no less I'm sure.

CHAPTER TWO

When I first moved in with the daft twat I would often wonder where the romance was and why there was no woman in the picture. Although to be honest it seemed there had been a few and he certainly wasn't a shy boy. As I hadn't even seen him with one I convinced myself that no way would I ever be jealous of another woman. When that day arrived I was incensed and had I been given time to think about it maybe I would have come round to the idea but I had no idea at all. The day began suspiciously because what was usually the norm all of a sudden did not seem to be happening. Dad and I always shared a bath and washed each other's backs, he was in the bath and suds

everywhere and I cart wheeled into the bathroom
ready to dive in. He put his hand out and
stopped me and I was confused. I was even
more confused when I realised he was shaving
his armpits and chest area. I'd never seen him
do this before. This was not his usual manly
behaviour. I was seeing a feminine side to him
and I hurriedly checked in the bedroom that he
didn't have a ball gown or summer frock on the
bed. "Shaving his armpits! What the fuck was
that all about"?

The rest of the day consisted of him
squirting after shave or deodorant on himself at
fifteen minute intervals. Slow it down son! What
about your carbon footprint? I felt a little
neglected for the biggest part of the day but just
put it down to him having a weird spell due to his
new tablets. I certainly felt pushed out when he
went to put his coat on and I was wagging my tail
at the door and he made it clear that I wasn't
going. He was going to leave the light and the

19

TV on for me! His phone rang and listening to the conversation it was clear he had himself a "hot date" and from us being inseparable, I was now to be left indoors alone.

I was not amused at all and joked to myself will he be taking "The Others" out with him to meet her or leaving them with me to play chess. I flicked through the TV stations after he had left but it was no good because the jealousy had me in a strangle hold and I couldn't think straight. I paced up and down the living room all night and then I heard the sound of a taxi door shutting and laughter coming up the stairwell from TWO people.

Not a shy girl then I thought as I pretended to be asleep on the settee and she almost fell on top of me in her drunken state. "Oh" she said "You never told me you had a dog"! What! I was raging now! By the sounds of it I hadn't even been mentioned once all night.

"How cute is HE"? was her next comment as I rolled over onto my back to make it clear to her that there was certainly nothing HE about me. I displayed all of my mimmim in its finest glory for her to see but was mortified to see she had begun to unfasten Dad's zip. "OMFG" I didn't know where to look or put myself as I froze on the spot. I think Dad realised because he very quickly took her out of the room and up the stairs to the bedroom that I usually slept in. I didn't even catch her name, she was such a fast worker but I stopped thinking that way instantly when I began to have a reality check and realised that I didn't want to know her name. Instead I wanted her gone. This girl was a threat with a capital T and had to go. I sulked for a while on the settee and couldn't get to sleep because of noises from above which didn't leave a lot to the imagination I can assure you.

I suddenly heard footsteps coming down the stairs and excitedly thought it may be Dad until I realised it was "The Hussy" coming to raid the fridge. I cringed when she walked past without any pants on and I could hear her gulping the milk in the fridge. Must be thirsty work I thought all the upstairs "cuddling"; still seething with jealousy. On her way back up the stairs she stopped to light a cigarette and put her final nail in her coffin by saying "are you okay there MISTER"? That was the final straw! We would never get on and I was sure of that. Round two more noises from the upper floor and out of politeness, I decided to let them finish their seedy little soiree and I would be up to meet you. I knew it wouldn't take him long to go to sleep and I had every intention of sticking myself between them on the pillow and going to sleep with my cute little arse in her face so that come the morning there would no doubt in her mind that the HE was in fact a SHE.

I'd never known myself be like this because I'm usually a cuteness overload for

22

everyone. A very small miniature Jack Russell but here I was showing very different emotions and if this continues I would need to start taking the split personality cocktail myself.!. I dragged the trampoline to the door that led me up to the stairs and was that angry I made contact with the handle on the first bounce and off I went up the stairs very stealthily so as not to wake either of them up. I stood in something wet with my paws on the way up the stairs and dragged it into the bathroom and discovered it was the briefest pair of panties you could ever come across. They were about as thin as a Rizla paper and I was tempted to flush them down the toilet. However, I decided that being as "Silly Bollox" never got much sex I would let him keep them as a trophy but unfortunately she would not be here again after tonight to wear them again. I would make sure of that!

I did a handspring up onto the bed and crawled up and had a good look at their faces to check if they were asleep. To my surprise I discovered that she was quite pretty but if anything that only confirmed that she really was likely to be a big threat. I made myself comfortable and sat my arse on her face for the rest of the evening and then just waited for "Silly Bollox" to wake me up for my regular morning stroll. Now it seemed even that routine had changed because he decided on having a bath first. She was still asleep and he reached over to kiss her head and whispered "I will save the water for you"! Yes you bastard, you used to say that to me but now it looks as if I am third in the pecking order. I could hear him singing and whistling in his bath the daft twat and I laughed recalling him shaving his arm pits. What a soppy twat and it would be fun letting his mates know somehow. But for now there were more pressing matters to deal with and I found the panties where I had left them and placed them over my head like an armed robber with a balaclava and I started to nuzzle myself next to "The Hussy's" head and eventually in her half asleep state she motioned to kiss "Silly Bollox" and planted her lips right on to her soiled panties and screamed and about brought the house down. From that moment I had her, every time she moved in any direction I growled very silently but made it clear that she should feel unsafe and threatened. She gathered her clothes together as quickly as she could and scurried down the steps with me close behind her still growling until she made her exit out of the flat and down the stairwell still only half dressed.

I was beside myself laughing because once I was out on the landing and waving her goodbye I realised I had still got the panties over my head ha-ha. I heard him shouting from the bathroom "are you awake yet Janet"? So at last I knew her name now, forget Janet you little Casanova I thought. "Get down here and get some fucking breakfast on the go" I thought. I put the panties on the coffee table to make it appear Janet had left them as a treat and the way he was caressing them fondly I had visions of seeing him wearing them over the coming weeks the soppy twat. "Enough" I thought put them in the washing machine; let's eat and go and have some exercise.

For the rest of the morning every spare moment I would him catch looking at his phone for miscalls or messages. He was funny to watch but it's quite easy for me to change his depressing mood because when I fed him his medication I just doubled him up on a blue pill and took away a red one and watched his eyes roll and spin till it was jackpotjoy.com. While his brain was addled on the settee I danced on the coffee table with the pants on my head singing "Juicy Janet's gone" and my Dad saying "what you doing Stella and who is Janet"? Exactly that dearest Daddy "who the fuck is Janet". Janet is no more, history; fun while it lasted. It had shown me a different side to me though, a nasty side I didn't think I had. I didn't feel guilty about what I had done though because for the last ten years I had my routine and in my heart I knew that Juicy Janet was likely to say "ugh you don't let your dog sleep on the bed do you"? That's what most women are like I suppose so in future it's going to be much easier to visit Trumps America than to get an overnight pass to sleep in Dads bedroom.

At his age he shouldn't be greedy anyway and that little bit of action should keep him smiling until I give him the heads up that he can do it again so he don't get frustrated. I know the signs, I'm a female and if I spot anyone sniffing round him while we are at the pub or wherever then I create a scene or a situation and we have to leave before any romance and little love birds twitter around him like in the cartoons. It's not like he is some sort of Tom Hardy and I will constantly be fighting all of you women off but I'm making it quite clear that "Silly Bollox" is not on the market.

To be honest I'm doing you all a favour because he can be very scary when he goes in "schizo mode". When I was listening to the loud bangs and noises from Juicy Janet to be honest I checked that all of his weapons were downstairs, the noises were that loud I feared for her safety. But "Silly Bollox" had been a good boy and just took his "weapon" of choice with him. Juicy Janet might have thought she was going to be Cleopatra eating grapes but not in this flat lady and he is lucky I didn't jump in the bath and shove the loofah up his arse.

CHAPTER THREE

Lots of people have been saying for a long time that we are a good double act and that one of us should write another book. Well that rules "Silly Bollox" out because he is getting blinder by the day. He waves at plenty of people that he shouldn't and calls them by name, when it looks nothing like the person who he thinks it is.

Oh the struggle is getting real with him and I can be classed as his assistance dog. It may sound a crazy title but that's exactly what I've been giving him for year's is lots of assistance. Apparently, I can't claim any allowance for all that I do for him when most nights I could scream with all of the day's events. He is going blind, starting to also suffer with his

29

hearing and last but not least he is stark raving bonkers and so the book writing is best if it's left to me for now.

We works as a team and will still split the proceeds anyway as we have always done. It's the only time we have ever earned any legal money lately, when we have written books because this will be our fifth offering. We have done factual, fiction and comedy to prove that we can write anything.

In between books we have had to get up to a few shady antics to survive. We have tried the living off the land routine, where I'm meant to be a hunter and Dad put a net over one hole and pointed to the other hole saying "go girl, get in". I just looked at him gone out thinking you stupid man. I'm not getting in any hole, it will be filthy down there and I'm fucked if I'm breaking one of my nails. Not at all Mister, if you don't mind I'd rather not get down any dark hole. I've read online about terriers needing to be dug out of holes and I suppose that's where the saying comes from. I will tell you now Stella Ginnelly will NOT be getting dug out of any hole.

I'd bumped into a rabbit one time in the woods and he seemed more startled than me but seemed a friendly enough chap. At the time I didn't even know what it was but once I got home and looked it up on Google it and it came up RABBIT, I couldn't catch my breath. A rabbit is meant to be my sworn enemy and I'm sorry but I just didn't get it. All of the whole hunting palaver was not my cup of tea and if we needed food that badly I would just as soon shoplift it to put it on the table. I'd got all that off to an art form anyway because I was that small I could waltz past even the sharpest store detective who wouldn't be taking much notice of the floor area. I would have my harness on and then at the top end of it I would tuck something in it like it like a tin of corned beef. Then walk out with that stuck up and on my back, I probably looked like a smaller version of an Indian elephant with the seating on its back.

The problem was I had run out of places to go because "Silly Bollox" had been banned everywhere and even now has to walk miles and miles to do even an honest shop because he is barred at all the local ones.

Believe it or not he had got a fixation about stealing different coloured bottles of hair conditioner and shampoo and he hasn't got a single hair on his head. It had become an obsession with him and in the bathroom there were fifty seven different shampoos and conditioners'. On this fateful day the Store Detective said politely "excuse me Sir, have you got something in your pocket you shouldn't have"? I was watching from the doorway of the supermarket as my Dad inquired innocently "like what"? The Store Detective had done his homework and replied "uum pear shampoo maybe"? L.O.L. With that the game was up and he pulled it out and was told he would be barred from the store for life and even then Dad tried to save face in front of the people watching by saying, he was glad because the prices were atrocious ha-ha. Everybody observing must have thought what the fuck you are doing with shampoo when you are bald? Most of them would have been thankful for the diversion, as it gave them the opportunity to sneak out with joints of meat or steaks down their trousers. I quickly ran in and grabbed my favourite block of cheese in all of the confusion.

Working class people have their backs to the wall more and more and nearly always due to the introduction of a Tory government. We were no different and finding ourselves suffering austerity, using Food Banks which Dad was far too proud to use on a regular basis. So one of us had to think up another way for us to survive using our wits and if it that took us down an illegal path then so be it because it was about survival.

I put a Stone Roses beanie hat on to hide my identity and I would shimmy through the estate with a pouch around my neck and a very tiny miner's torch on my head so I could check that all the notes were genuine because any dodge notes would be deducted from my wages and then rightly or wrongly I would drop little sachets of cocaine off to people. Supply and demand, I had just seen it as the exact same as someone delivering a take away meal. Except my customers would not be eating; I hadn't even told Dad what I was doing. I kept hiding the money and I would have told him at a later date when we had enough to get us by. He had been waiting THREE YEARS for a Personal Independence Payment (PIP) assessment, a staggering three years! Shame on this government and all of the hardship they put people through.

Things had been ticking over nicely and I had been earning a decent amount every weekend for perhaps four months and was even preparing to stop being in the thick of if it all. I shuffled by the local shops one evening still wearing my beanie hat and sensed immediately something was not right; as I spotted a very unfamiliar breed of dog for our estate and the dog came and sat by me and wagged its tail and I'd watched enough Border Control programmes on TV to realise that it was a drugs dog and obviously police would be close by. Luckily I was a very fit little dog and all that swimming had strengthened my legs and I was off like a bullet out of a gun and the only one that could even remotely keep up with me was the police dog; until I turned and threatened to chew his face off. He soon retreated with a whimper and definitely didn't have the stomach for a fight.

I had got away but it was really only temporary and I had to guess how much they did already know, how long had they witnessed my activities? I hid behind some garages while I gathered my thoughts but instead I should have used my time to get away from the area because before I knew it the full beam of the helicopter was on me and my hat and I found myself under arrest.

At the station while I waited to be booked in I noticed the security was very slack and especially where the big double doors opened. I slid along the surface like Torvill and Dean the ice skaters and my nails being a little longer than usual thankfully just slid me straight out of the doors and onto the car park. I hit the street running but even so I kept falling over laughing at the thought of my arresting officer going to book me in and just placing his hand on an empty hat with nothing or nobody under it. That thought had me in hysterics until I realised they would have my DNA from the hat should they find me again.

I never went home until I had gathered that at no time had they been there since the arrest or the escape so they didn't know as much as I thought they did. I now had visions of me in a half yellow half denim escapee outfit, like Dads friend Charlie Bronson Salvador has to wear for escaping from custody or being a high risk prisoner. How much trouble was I in, how many years would they hold me? For fucks sake Dads friend was in his forty-fourth year now and had never killed anyone and it's the biggest injustice in our legal system. Successive Home Secretaries have overlooked Charlie time and again, even though huge amounts of people from different generations sign petitions time after time and nobody seems in the least bit concerned. It can't be allowed to continue and I agree with Dad that Charlie should be released UNLESS I'm going in his cage next and if that's the case then fuck it I'm not going to sign the petition L.O.L. Can anyone even begin to imagine serving forty-four years in a cell? It doesn't bear thinking about to be honest but I'm in the shit and can't stop thinking about it because every copper in Nuneaton is out looking for me.

I wasn't going to be able to hide forever, so I had to think on my feet, it might be better if I surrender myself back into custody in the company of the family solicitor Chris Pendle of Rotherham & Co., The Quadrant Coventry. Chris had perhaps made his first million representing Dads family of six brothers and four sisters down the years on lots of varied criminal offences and obviously not guilty of any them. I had emailed Chris without Dad knowing and arrangements had been made to surrender at a time convenient to ourselves within the next few days. It wasn't like there was a story to work out or nothing because I would simply be repeating NO COMMENT over and over again which Chris would also be encouraging me to do.

It was bad enough going to jail at any time but if you should ever find yourself on an exercise yard through the words from your own tongue it will crucify your mind throughout the sentence. Anyway, I had been brought up well and I would never confess even if they tried to beat it out of me. If they ever tried throwing one of their dogs in my cell they would need the first aid box when I threw it back out; because I absolutely flourish fighting big dogs, the bigger the better. My name's Stella Ginnelly; it's NO COMMENT all the way and I will fight the biggest dog you have in the station. I won't need to Chris Pendle is a good solicitor and I will be on bail in no time.

CHAPTER FOUR

I never told Dad anything; I set off early morning to meet up with Chris on the car park opposite the Justice Centre to discuss the charges that I may face. We went into the station that was within the Justice Centre and after exchanging courteous pleasantries. I found myself in an interview room with the never changing scenario you see in all of the police situations in the movies. My Solicitor and I are sitting alongside each other and the good cop and bad cop duo facing us at the other side of the table firing a barrage of questions. "Where did you get the drugs from"? Enquired good cop, "no comment" was my constant reply or complete stony silence. Because I knew they had nothing on me after they had offered me a lesser charge of possession of a controlled drug rather than the more serious charge of intent to supply. If they had the evidence to prove it they wouldn't be playing the bargaining game already and considering they had not actually found any in my possession they would struggle in a courtroom to gain a solid conviction so I was prepared to contest everything.

My Solicitor left the room with one of the detectives and I was left with the bad cop with the stony face telling me that in the old days he would have beat a confession out of me or fabricated his own statement against me. I simply smiled and winked at him because he and I both knew that since the introduction of the CCTV at almost every angle of every room including the cells that police brutality was kept to a minimum in the present era. I had heard Dad telling his friends of the beatings he suffered as a young child; it sickened me that he went through all of what he did at the hands of these Pillars of

Society (SIC). I could readily understand where a lot of his mental illness stemmed from, as he was left with very violent images in his head of what he endured and from being a very placid young boy. His encounters with these people led him to believe that violence was the normal way to be.

He had travelled up to Kirklevington in Yarm in Teesside paid for by the BBC to give an interview regarding his own violent treatment at the hand of very sadistic guards who are presently on bail and likely to face charges due to the excessive violence. This brutality on a very large scale towards young teenage boys, whom nobody had believed at the time but now for the first time were being listened too. Dad had been perhaps fifteen years of age and had been strangled until he blacked out by one of the Officers and thrown in a heap on the floor. Then after water was thrown in his face and he came round a little he was kicked hard in his stomach until he was retching on the floor. He was made to pull a plough up and down fields with some of the other prisoners and most weeks would never pass without a black eye or a fat lip. In today's more tolerant society actions like this are not permitted and this evil bastard across from me was aware of that and when I jumped down from my chair and raised one of my legs he joked "that scared you didn't it"? In reality I had grown bored of his threats and gently lowered my back paws and urinated on his pristine floor and again winked at him; just so he realised that I hadn't done it out of FEAR. I had done it out of bravado you very silly man.

Chris came back in the room and it was plain to see with the eye contact and slight shrug of the shoulders by one of the Officers; that I would not be revealing what they wanted to know. Of course I knew who provided all of the cocaine but no way would I give up my source to them. It was Pablo Escobar and no way would I give them his name. I didn't even get bailed to a later date as it was concluded that I had no charges to face and that was the end of the matter. Although they would be keeping the Stone Roses hat It was a loss I would have to take on the chin.

I'd got that special when I went up Heaton Park in Manchester with Dad and his mates, Granty, Gaz Duncan, Cory, Spud, James, Anton, Jack and Spud's pretty bit of skirt Dani. We took Manchester over for the night although the others had £80 hotel rooms my Dad and Granty just roughed it in a car park in Deansgate, Manchester. They couldn't see any point paying for a bed when they weren't going to be sleeping. I felt like the luckiest dog ever to be there for the Roses re-union gig. We had the best night ever, with the best cocaine ever and it was just one of the most memorable nights I'd ever had. My mind had just drifted back to the occasion until a voice said "So do you understand the consequences of any further arrests" and snapped me out of it, while I watched the Desk Sergeant roll off his customary lecture. I was already making for the door humming "I want to be adored" quite loudly and they knew I was winding them up and were happy to have got rid of me to the other side of the door before I went into a few verses from "she bangs the drums" which could have been quite fitting in my case. Me and Chris parted company on the car park.

I just had a little stroll into town where I was quite well known to be honest and I was in no rush to head home. As I had a few things to celebrate since my release, so I thought a few hours in town wouldn't harm. How wrong could I be because later when I approached the flat it was obvious a situation was developing? I was laughing to myself as to how there never seemed to be a dull moment in these flats. The laugh would soon disappear from my face upon realising "Silly Bollox" was the central focus of the unfolding event that had only just begun. So

I may be able to rescue the situation before any police or other official parties became involved. A quick review of the situation made me realise that due to my late arrival back home "Silly Bollox" had not been given his medication for the day because of my absence and I hastened into the flat as quickly as I could because there was not a moment to spare. The daft one that we all love had begun to froth at the mouth while he stood there completely naked except for his socks and his hand around the throat of his uninvited guest who had knocked his door. Who was in panic mode and kept saying over and over "Jesus Christ I only asked him did he want to swap energy supplier" while stating that he worked for EON. I assured the man to stay calm and he would soon be able to carry on his duties and knock the other flats but the look on his face told me that the very minute that Dad let go of his throat, the last thing he would be doing would be knocking other doors in these flats. In actual fact

I doubted that he would ever, knock any door EVER again.

Yes of course, it was possible to meet some lovely people who would put the kettle on and even bring a saucer full of biscuits out BUT was it worth it if on the flip side you encountered a lunatic in just a pair of socks and holding a machete telling you about "The Others" who were in charge. Never in is wildest dreams could he have imagined this scenario and he probably promised himself that if he ever got out of this situation alive, that for the rest of his days he wouldn't give a toss about which energy supplier anybody at all was using. I had hastily emptied the capsules into a glass of milk, I got Dad to sit down gently and have a few sips and wait for a little composure to settle in and finally normality. I ushered the other neighbours away assuring them everything was fine and handed Dad some clothes to get dressed. The "Hostage" waited till both of Dads hands were full with the clothing and made good his escape; I would calculate the first 100 metres would have been close to a UK record. Dad and I shouted after him that he had left his clip board behind but somehow or other I don't think he would ever work for that company again.

I got Dad indoors and spent the rest of the day giving him more and more dosage until he finally seemed quite normal. Looking at him butter wouldn't melt in his mouth but he had a very lucky escape there because if the police had become involved he would have gone away for a very long time. As much as I am accustomed to looking after myself I wouldn't have fancied living in the flat alone.

He put his trainers on and it seemed that he fancied a little walk which was okay because at times like this I get some very good dog walks, right down the canal and through the woods. Off we went and were enjoying the stroll until "Silly

One" started making lots of real desperate faces and it soon became clear that it was due to the quick rush of all of his medication. He needed the toilet and could hold it no longer and ran and squatted exactly where he stood and lowered himself down and defecated something similar to a cow pat. I found it quite amusing and laughed at the chaotic picture and also the noises he continued to make. Although, it soon transpired the noises were due to another matter. It turned out when he had lowered himself the bulk of his arse cheeks had been lowered onto stinging nettles and his posterior now looked like a big blood orange and he was suffering a lot of discomfort. He made it clear the walk was over for today and we needed to get back to the flat. He made a lot of pained noises all the way back and when we got home. I ran upstairs so that he wouldn't see me laughing at his expense. When I thought I had suitably composed myself to go back downstairs the sight that greeted me made me collapse in hysterical fits of laughter. He had the bowl from the kitchen sink filled with frozen vegetables and peas from the freezer and he was sat in the middle of the living room with his bare arse sat in the middle of the frozen produce. Why oh why at these times do I not have access to a Smartphone because a photo of him sat that way would make a fortune? I couldn't stop falling over laughing; it was the funniest sight I'd ever seen and strangely enough "Silly Bollox" would eat those self same frozen vegetables within the next few days.

Our life was constantly like this and packed with fun. I don't know which was redder, his face with embarrassment or his arse cheeks. Ha-ha.

CHAPTER FIVE

The image wouldn't leave me for days and the comic content couldn't get any better because he stayed sat on the bowl reading his newspaper for the next few hours. Just when I thought things could not get any funnier I opened the door one day to Dads friend who was even nuttier than him. He shall remain unnamed but had a spell in the Territorial Army and picked up the name Rambo for obvious reasons.

You would not dare say in his presence "them fuckers over there look a bit dodgy and weird" because within the next five minutes they would all be headed for a hospital bed because of him hearing you say it. He always seemed to be on the run from the police for one thing or another. I listened into a phone conversation between him and Dad. Where Rambo was on the run and hiding in Skegness and got himself some seasonal work handing out some leaflets, promoting a new fish and chip shop that had opened BUT he was dressed in a big outfit of a cod fish. L.O.L. He shouted down the phone that he had to go because he had just seen his boss come around the corner and he had to race out of the phone box and flip the cod's head back down over his face.

Talk about laugh, you couldn't make this sort of stuff up. In our life's stories like this are very much priceless. We all have our share of doom and gloom with the deaths we endure but stories such as the above level things out a little.

Rambo was and still is a very good darts player. He has another nickname with it on the back of his shirt BULLSEYE and a very big dartboard on his back. He has won many competitions and had a normal spell in his life just doing a bit of "darting". When he got asked to leave or threw out of one of our local pubs he returned later and threw some petrol bombs in the place. Not exactly a nine dart finish but his aim was true with the petrol bombs as he scorched all the walls and windows LOL. Obviously, he would need to go into hiding again and he had recently watched a programme about people panning for gold in Scotland. Off he went with a rucksack, map and a riddle to find the gold just like the gold rush in the old western movies.

Obviously it was a different time of being on the run and different incident but Dad would laugh insanely thinking of Bull's-eye/Rambo panning for gold dressed up as a cod up in Scotland. God knows what the local natives would have made of Deano because he is a one off unique character who never fails to bring laughter to the table. He definitely gives Dad a good run for his money and his latest venture is not for the faint hearted. This is because Rambo now thinks he is psychic. He can predict all about anybody in a room and he is now wearing all of the bling with the mystical hidden eye. He can sense everything about you just by staring in your direction. He is in touch with others from around the world and they have got the lot of us weighed up and under control. I keep watching for him flying past the window playing Quiditch with the rest of the gang.

Dad always says this is the best Estate he has ever lived on for characters. It makes him feel at home because he is nuts himself and it's like being in one big asylum. The one thing that can be said about Rambo is that he can always be called on to bring a bit of muscle to the table. He should be on the same tablets as Dad but seems to have gone untreated for the best part of his life. It don't help that he is quite deaf because it's the same routine every time. Dad shouts from the kitchen "do you want a can Rambo" and he just stares at the TV and don't hear a thing.

I just jump up on the coffee table and watch the pair of them, Dad talking about "The Others" and Rambo not hearing a word. It's comedy gold with this pair! I get one of my toys and start to rag it about and Rambo always says "Jack Russell's are mad aren't they"? You couldn't make it up. He says "I'm mad". listen up Rambo you and Dad are the fucking lunatics just like half of this estate.

What I can't understand is if you are a psychic now then how come you don't know where the gold is to be found and please, please, please on your next expedition take "Silly Bollox" with you and give me a lengthy break and even dress him as a fish. I'd love to stand at the bus stop and wave you both off and tell you both not to come back until you have made yourselves your first million. In fact it would be a good idea to round the rest of them up on the estate like One Flew over the Cuckoo's Nest. If Jack Nicholson lived around here he would be the sanest one and that says a lot about some of you.

Three asylums my Dads been in and had strait jackets wrapped around him and if I didn't live here with him he would have been marked down for electric shock treatment years ago. One of the mysteries of the universe is how the fuck Rambo hasn't been wrapped up tight in one and put in a padded cell. I'm sure that between the pair of you, you could manage to fill a mini bus up just from this estate. All the way up to Scotland you could all sing the wheels on the bus go round and round. There's gold in them there hills ladies and gentlemen. L.O.L.

I didn't even want to know why Rambo had called and I set off out to have a little mooch out down the canal by myself and left Dad talking to "The Others" and Rambo just tilting his head from side to side trying to determine if somebody was even talking or not. This was my life

56

everyday to be honest so I just soldiered on. I didn't call him "Silly Bollox" for the fun of it. So if we had a visitor it gave me an opportunity to go out and have a little "me" time while Dad had company and I just had to hope and pray that no other door knocker came asking "do you want to change your energy supplier". If I was out by myself roaming the estate, after a while dad would stand in the bay window looking to see me. Once I came back into the area and I saw he was fully clothed then any worries soon went away. The problem with the bay window is it is by a very busy main road and on more than one occasion he has stood naked waving at everyone on the school run.

It's an interesting life people I can assure you of that, but I'd never swap with anyone because I had lived at perhaps four or five different addresses and sometimes I was shown kindness and I was happy but before you knew it I was moved again and never had any consistency in my life.   Until I met this mad one and now I could never live nowhere else.   He takes me everywhere I have done thousands of miles with him and been to ever coastline and swam in every sea imaginable. I sense when the love is real and nobody could have a better Dad than me.   He turned me from being a little unwanted dog on a back yard to the most famous dog in Nuneaton with my own Facebook page with thousands of friends, STELLA G. GINNELLY check it out for yourselves.   When I go down town with him I am never tied up unless it's market day and busy.   He lets me run free and nearly every single person in the town knows who I am and if I get left outside a shop people come and talk to me. A few lonely people in the town have said they are house bound most of the time and they wait each day for my Facebook stories and adventures and it raises their spirits and makes their day.

I am a funny little dog of that I am sure and Dad tells these people that I belong to the entire town. Everyone is a part owner and he makes sure I feel proper loved. Nobody ever saw me on a backyard in the old days but now everywhere I go I hear people shout "here's Stella" and I feel so loved, proud and wanted that I feel as if I could live forever. None of that would ever have been possible without the love shown by my "Silly Bollox" of a Dad. We just basically need each other I suppose and our bond now is unbreakable. He worries when I go out alone and he had bought me a collar with STELLA GINNELLY, CALDWELL COURT on a little disc but the daft twat forgot that he had me chipped over at Coventry PDSA to this address and the miles I've walked with him and the street corners I've pissed on I could never ever get lost.

On the slight chance I ever did it would be like the film LASSIE COME HOME because I would cross mountains and rivers to find him again. He might be a nutcase but he is my nutcase and diamond encrusted. Rescued me when I most needed him, I was going insane on that backyard and I've definitely seen how he also was losing the plot alone in here. Mental illness though is nothing to be ashamed of; it just means that you're a little quirky, not wired like the rest, around the hat rack. Use whatever term you want but in reality you are just a little out of sync and that's all well and good while it's manageable. But all of the young suicides lately are becoming crazy and at them low periods I wish every one of them had access to mine or Dads pages and could just have a laugh and climb out of that hole. I've heard Dad talk to others (REAL others not "The Others") L.O.L. and he has been in THREE different suicide situations and revived in the back of an ambulance so he wouldn't just talk bluster to you because he, himself, has been in the exact same situations and knows all about the BLACK DOG. It's a black hole we fall in and a hand is needed at that very time because no way can you climb out yourself. He knows, He has been treated for mental illness his whole life and yet he is the funniest person you would ever meet so work that one out!

I wouldn't swap him for the world and now as the band Faithless say WE BECOME ONE. We are a team and we will bring laughter into any of your sad situations now we accept you as friends. Come and visit this daft twat though so I can get out more by myself.

CHAPTER SIX

We are at our happiest when the heavens open and the heavier the deluge the better because we will stay out in the rain for hours. Long walks down the canal and no likelihood of bumping into anyone. It's absolutely perfect as I run and splash through every puddle and occasionally I dive in the canal and swim on my back while I juggle my tennis balls.

I go deaf for some strange reason when I hit water but it matters little because Dad just marches onwards talking to himself or "The Others" if we have brought them with us. I sometimes run along in front and then race up on to one of the bridges and so one of my Tom Daley dives and spin in mid air. I just have an obsession with water I can always be found in it day after day and there's no harm in that to be honest. Even the Vet told Dad that swimming would help ease the arthritic pain I got in my back legs from time to time. I run from bridge to bridge so that I am in front at all times and can keep a safe eye on my Dad. This same situation goes on for mile after mile and I would safely say that I am the fittest dog on the estate because many days we do a ten mile round trip without even seeing one person in the torrential rain.

It is very much back to nature and one man and his dog and these days will always be among some of my favourite memories especially when you considered that in my early years I was limited to a small yard for exercise. My life was complete with this man and I was a happy little dog leading a much fulfilled life.

Everybody on the Estate would greet us warmly because for all of Dads mental health problems he was a very well respected man and highly thought of by the young or old Residents in the neighbourhood. The young children would rush to watch me while Dad went in any of the local shops because they knew that he would come out throwing packets of sweets everywhere. In reality I would never need watching, I would never be placed on a lead and I would sit outside the shop and even if Dad was in there until the following day I would be sat in the exact same spot. However, Dad wanted everyone to feel they were a part of my life and if I'm honest I didn't mind all of the little hands stroking my head and pampering me because it made me feel special with all of them sat on the floor around me. I would feel like a very loved and special dog.

Some of my funniest moments would be outside of them shops because Dad would come out and have all of the kids jumping up and down to get their treats. All of their parents would know him by name and have no problem with their kids taking sweets from Dad because he was no stranger. Also they had all been told by Dad or their parents to tell Dad if there were any bullying problems or if they needed any help.

It's nice having a community like that and that's exactly how Dad had grown up in Yorkshire, when he was a small boy.

I would love listening to his stories and I thought it very unfair that dogs couldn't have a longer life span because I would have loved to have been at the side of "Silly Bollox" for the whole of his life but even being a part of it for the short life span I had was well worth it for the fun he packed in for me. Even the days he came out of the shop with one of the Jack Daniels mixers in a can, that he had taken a liking for would turn out to be funny.

He would try to teach the kids about hopscotch and they would look at him gone out because they already had hopscotch frames painted on all of their school playgrounds. But off he went doing his hop on one leg and a double stamp and back to the hop and never once spilling a drop from his can and I would cover my eyes and didn't bear to look L.O.L. Any of the parents coming to the shop for provisions would laugh and say "are you looking after him Stella"? I would laugh at the irony of that. Looking after him was in fact around the clock 24/7 task.

We would hang about the shops, as it would be easier for him to keep popping into the shop once his can was empty. I would think don't get going home yet children because just another two cans of his favourite tipple and you will witness the funniest hop you have ever seen and standing on his one free leg would become increasingly more difficult. I would spot the signs and get him home before he had a fall and he would definitely lose his game of hopscotch.

Most days I would need to bed him down anyway in the afternoon for one of his "nanny naps" when he would grab an hour and a little power nap. It was fine by me because I could have a little sprawl on the settee with the remote and have a little catch up TV. I would watch my favourite film TED about the man's teddy bear coming to life and being quite grown up and rude and it reminds me of many aspects of my own life except mine is much more comical.

Sometimes we would take some of the kids with us on our safaris and they would love it; it's got to be better than them sat playing computer games and worrying about Health and Safety issues and children just not having a childhood no more.

I don't think Dad ever grew up anyway and he has tied oil drums around planks of wood and made a raft and I've had the time of my life testing it out with him on the water. I'd never feel in any danger anyway because for sure I'm an Olympic swimmer BUT "Silly Bollox" can't swim a stroke and so I'm just putting it out there for all of you parents in case he ever says to you "I will take all of the kids and build a raft" L.O.L.

At these times I suppose Health and Safety measures are required because otherwise I've got visions of Dad in the middle of the canal on his raft with his can of Jack Daniels and all the kids screaming and swimming for the shore while he salutes and goes down with his ship.

They would be safe; I would rescue the little ones if it ever happened. Then while we're safely on the canal tow path we could all take photos of the daft twat going down with his ship because the water in the canal is only about four foot deep and he would be saluting but the water would only go up to his chest. But I think the same as him that the kids of today don't take enough risks or have any of the fun that they could have if they just turn that games console off and get out of the bedroom.

Dad knew where there was a rope swing in the woods and it seemed we were the only ones that ever used it. I would jump up and sink my teeth into the knot and I would get spun round and round and this would be much better fun for the kids, but we doubted they even knew it was there.

Dad got all his medals for injuries as a kid from his broken arm, fingers or stitches and it was part and parcel of growing up. He would be up the hospital that often that he would get invited to the Christmas party for kids and even Santa had said to him "I better not play with you or I may need to be treated at the hospital". He didn't know how true that statement was but I would have loved to have been there and been his little puppy at the time when he was a small child himself and I'm sure I would have needed X-rays or stitches myself ha-ha.

He must have always been a dog lover because I heard stories of an Alsatian type dog called Karl who he would tie to his push bike and let run alongside while he played or ran errands for people and the local butcher would knock the window and give him a big bag of bones for the dog. His Uncle Billy had brought it home with him from the army when he had been in Hong Kong and Dad had the dog from being a pup. I was a little jealous but was pleased Dad had got fun from a different dog when he was little. Where he had lived as a child I had listened to many stories while he talked to his friends and one of the most awful tales ever concerned a dog.

One of Dads neighbours had given Dad sixpence in pre-decimal money to take a dog for a walk, to meet somebody or so he thought. But ust down from the neighbourhood, by the railway bridge in Westtown, Dewsbury was a little council depot across from the John F. Kennedy public house and it is a memory that has haunted him. He gave the note to the man in the yard and that could and should have been the end of the matter as he took the dog. But the evil bastard that he was he had placed lots of pads on the dog; He had closed the door and then told Dad to look through the window of the room. Dad witnessed the dog writhing and burning with the electric current running through it and he was rooted to the spot and mouth wide open as the horrible bloke dragged the carcass out and threw it on to a pile of what he now knew to be other dead dogs. Dad had ran all the way home crying and had thrown up and thrown the sixpence away. He didn't want it; it was blood money in his eyes. He couldn't blame the woman who had given it to him, because no way would she have thought a small child would witness what my Dad just had. Dad would try to always walk the long way round after that and never go near that place ever again. What had really shocked him was the amount of dogs that were there and the last thing they would ever see would be this sadistic bastard who simply threw them about like rag dolls.

Nowadays there are more humane ways to put a dog to sleep but Dad has never been able to forget what he saw at perhaps eight years of age and many times he would hope and pray that man was not a parent or a dog owner. Out of all bad comes good and its maybe this one incident that made him love animals the way he does and I get the benefit of that because I am treated like Royalty and I want for nothing. I have the best food and I get regular grooms, even when and most of the time he can't afford it because he always puts me first; I am so thankful to have him. To the bastard who done that to him as a small child I would love to sink my teeth firmly into your ankle or I hope you had a slow and painful death. It back fired as it created a man who gave me that much love and always will that both of us have constant smiles on our faces and can't wait to see each other when we wake on a morning. As soon as he opens his eyes I dive on him with my tail spinning like the police helicopter. Every single day with him is worth waking to.

CHAPTER SEVEN

Absolutely fantastic, I thought out loud. Oh I've been here before and I recognise the signs which are not to difficult to spot in all honesty being as how "Silly Bollox" is doing all the moves in the kitchen and singing "Hey Macarena" at the top of his voice spinning round and round.

I raced up the stairs to confirm it and sure enough, the suitcase was out of the cupboard and essentials stacked around it. It could only mean one thing and that was if the passport was in use then Stella Ginnelly was going to be dumped in the flat alone with "The Others" and I was livid. This happened often with foreign holidays and Dad and his mates booking up on last minute holidays and off they went with barely any notice. They were welcome, they were all as daft as each other I whispered to myself feeling quite jealous and pushed out. I couldn't complain really because I had been to every coastal area in the UK and had never been left behind if it was a UK holiday. It was just much more difficult to get out and into Europe which I couldn't understand because if they got a chance to meet me I'm sure we would all get along just fine. Cheeky bastards anyway, because I've more chance of catching rabies, from your mongrels than you would have from me. The problem is I do like to fight big dogs and I wouldn't fancy putting my teeth into one of them abroad unless it was for a little ohh la la!

I would never be left alone; at times like this I would have a little mini holiday myself because a lovely couple I know. Jo Gore and Steve Bell always look after me and I would have lots of love and cuddles with treats all day long. I would always have lot of laughs watching Steve thinking he was the dominant partner but Jo would clip him around his ear and put him in his place and he would go all quiet and his face would always make me giggle. It was a nice break for me staying with them every time and I'd always behave then I knew I could stay there again and sometimes it made more sense staying at home than travelling into Europe with "Silly Bollox".

Just off the top of my head I can recall him going to Rotterdam to watch England play Holland and it don't take him long to find trouble BUT ten minutes must be a bit of a record L.O.L. He had barely taken a sip of his first drink, when a tennis ball threw by Dutch supporters exploded in a cloud of smoke and sent shards of nails about. Oh trust only my Dad can be hit by a nail bomb upon arrival. Another time coming back from Crete he was accused of having a cigarette on the plane, he denied it and the Stewardess said the Captain was still deciding what to do. Dad had gone to sleep thinking it was all bluff however upon arrival at East Midlands Airport seven Police Officers boarded the plane and arrested him and took him to Coalville Police Station. After a taped interview and Dad taunting them about insufficient evidence. They eventually agreed with him and released him at four am in the morning. Still dressed in his holiday clothes of shorts and flip flops, they assured him that he wouldn't like the weather out there and they were indeed correct. They had thrown him out in a minus ten perhaps sort of a morning and Dad had to sit in a phone kiosk bear hugging himself for warmth; until someone finally got out of bed that could come and pick him up. The Police knew they could not charge him but played their Joker. A little bit of one-upmanship to teach Dad a lesson, which they hoped would improve his behaviour.

Alas on the very next jaunt to Tenerife a few Lucky Lucky Men got given a few slaps for taking advantage of my Dad and his friends' kindness. The last thing this pair would have felt that night was "Lucky Lucky" I'm guessing as they ended up in the back of an ambulance while Dad slept on the beach and his friend slept at the airport. They had got their clothes earlier and passports from the hotel so they split up and arranged to meet up at the airport the following morning. It was time for a cheap flight out of there and "Vamoose Amigos! Adios! He won't be in a rush to go there again.

So now do you all understand that it's definitely no big loss not getting out into Europe with this idiot, no way are you even remotely safe and I don't care what insurance you have took out. Going anywhere with "Silly Bollox" is like skating on thin ice. You are taking your life into your own hands. "Will you miss me Stella" he asked while he was still doing his version of the

Macarena and I doubted very much that I'd miss being with him because by now I knew the destination was Benidorm.

Oh dear! Ouch! I was more than sure that he, the others and his own "Others" could find trouble there, without a doubt; I would stake a million pound on it. Upon hearing the destination I was certainly relieved now to know I would be back in the UK laid at the feet of Jo and getting pampered and fed treats while we watched what we wanted and made Steve sit in a different chair and shut up about his favourite subject Liverpool. "Not another word Steve" Jo would say "or you will be up to bed" and he knew when to go quiet. I would wink at him to cheer him up a little and I would wonder if he sat here by the feet of Jo if I was not here.

They are going to be away for four days and I loved being round this pair and I could relax from being Dads Carer and have some me time with my favourite couple. Even when the laws change I'm not sure I would want to board a plane with Dad because all I have done is highlight a few incidents and trust me there are many, many more incidents. He had been made to sit on the forecourt of an Italian garage with his hands on his head with guns pointed at him by local Police. So why don't we have a vote here and now or conduct an online poll and ask people; who wants to go abroad with "Silly Bollox"? Make it a special treat for someone you don't really like L.O.L. I will even chip in and help towards the flight for someone.

So anyway it came as no surprise to anyone, least of all me, to hear that they had been stopped from boarding; while they had their hands and cases swabbed almost as soon as they left the airport bar full of Jack Daniels at six am in the morning and singing the Macarena. You couldn't make this shit up people. They are only two hours into the journey and been getting swabbed and lined up. God help Benidorm! The only reason the others were going was one was Dads brother and the other two hadn't even been told who the other person was (Dad) on the flight in case they cancelled their holiday L.O.L.

From a safety point of view there would be no risk to any of the other passengers through Dad smoking because he had stopped for the best part of a year now. Although he certainly had not stopped drinking and it was all about the Jack Daniels and coke now and he had progressed to the actions and lyrics of the "Birdy Song" now as he raced up and down the aisle doing all of the wing flapping motions whilst singing. Someone was relaying all of this back home by text message and also the captain was kept informed whilst I pictured it and found it funny; I also hoped that they remembered days and times for his medication. As the last thing other passengers would need is him stripping off out of the blue while doing the "Birdy Song".

It was a little off season at the hotel and a little quiet but amongst the residents there I could also imagine the hotel staff running a sweepstake. To pick out who they thought would be most difficult guests and I can picture them squealing with delight when they seen them four get out of the taxi at the front of the hotel and all of them wanting to throw a week's wage on this lot being the red hot favourites to win any trophy. It wouldn't take long to have it all confirmed because the first night Dad was fumbling about in the room wanting the bathroom, opened a door and upon seeing a lighted area oohed and aahed and set about reliving himself.

The problem was he was out in the hotel corridor and rumour had it he was stripped off and I fell off Jo's settee upon hearing this. I could imagine the desk staff at the hotel pointing to the CCTV and howling with laughter, especially, the ones who had placed money on them four being the rowdiest guests, for the next four days. Oh dear I thought, they haven't seen anything yet ha-ha. Once Dad had pissed up the wall, to be honest they were lucky he had not gone back into a completely different hotel room after.

In fact when they got a chance they should introduce Dad to the hotels Doctor just so they had a chance to meet early during their stay. Another good idea would have been to have a syringe conveniently on hand with the strongest tranquiliser known to man in it. He had been injected often enough in the bottom of his foot with Largactil so if he appears to be upsetting other guests take him out quickly before his behaviour worsens.

I laughed away to myself and this was just the confirmation that I needed that i had the more peaceful break out of the pair of us. I know all of the gossip from out there now but I'm sworn to secrecy as I'm sure you all know the rules, what happens in Benidorm stays in Benidorm.

The only clue I can give you is my sides have spilt on several occasions thinking about the daft twat that is my Dad, because I'd place a big bet that they won't be in no rush to get on a plane with him ever again L.O.L.

Just off the strip is a white building and Dads bladder is the weakest anyone could ask for and he pisses about six times an hour, walking back to the hotel he had begun to piss up against the white building. If you've been to Benidorm you will know that the building is the local Police Station. For once he was not spotted and had a bit of luck because at any other time the Desk Sergeant would have ran out and give him a few tickles in the ribs with his baton and there would have been no more Macarena for that day. They would have beaten him black and blue had they seen him. If they had checked at the hotel he was staying at and they had told them about him pissing up the hotel corridor it would have been game over for him. Brexit will be worth it just to stop this crazy fool from travelling.

CHAPTER EIGHT

Once he got back I readily admit that I do miss him when he is not about because life becomes very boring and pedestrian without the soft twat. Of course, I jump up to his shoulders and kiss and lick his face off and why wouldn't I? He is my Dad and I love him.

Because Dad had reached a certain age he was now exempt from paying bedroom tax, which had been proper crucifying us for years. We had struggled through using all the local food banks and not ashamed to admit it were either of us. It was basic staple food like rice and pastas and not the luxury shop that everyone was led to believe. All of the judgemental ones with the usual comments "well yes I'd like free food".

Some of you just don't seem to understand how this Tory Government have turned us against each other. People become jealous and nasty about any individual getting free shopping, which at a regular Food Bank amounts to emergency supplies to last three days. It's NOT a month's food which many of you seem to think and people are only allowed to use it for three times a year. I wish you all knew this when you criticise people.

In his position while he had worked he had given this Council in excess of £60,000 out of his wages for rent and had paid out of his own pocket for home improvements. The Council insisted he had to downsize to a one bedroom flat or pay a surplus of £14 a week for his empty bedroom. Can anyone stand and look him in the eye and say that's fair because plenty of people who work for the Council didn't agree with it.

People would help Dad find his shortfall and an organisation called Ediblelinks in Atherstone was a Godsend to Dad. I was over the moon and doing cartwheels because Sonya Johnson who masterminded the whole operation would not only provide people with food BUT animals also; I would get some beautiful food in my bowl proper gourmet dog food.

We should never have had to live like this in the first place but I would thank them, just as much as "Silly Bollox" because of how I was looked after as well. I'm only a miniature Jack Russell with a small voice that people wouldn't listen to and I try not to get political but I do have an urge to at least say FUCK THE TORIES.

Dad needed to call into the Town Hall and that would always start him off going all political .The lady at the desk always enjoyed bumping into Dad because he made her laugh but when we called in on this day and Dad had sores on the tip of his nose, she said "oh Mr Ginnelly you haven't been falling over have you"? Falling, falling? He couldn't stop laughing as he informed her he no longer had to pay Bedroom Tax and could afford to fly all around Europe instead L.O.L. Not quite, but at least he was not as poor as he had been.

They both laughed and joked with each other and she said she had missed seeing him call in and me because she loved seeing me. She would look after me while "Silly Bollox" went for yet another shout out. She would not have to wait for long to be seeing him again. He would be infuriated because the dirty tricks department had taken over and because they had reached the stage where he could no longer be evicted they would need another reason to get him out AND it transpired that he did not have permission for me STELLA GINNELLY to be in the flat. Can you fucking believe these people TEN YEARS I had been living here and they were saying that I am basically a squatter? I've chased every rat away from the bin area and Dads looked after all of the Residents in the flats and we work as a team but it appears the rats that need chasing are the ones who work for the Town Hall.

One time Dad tried to pretend one of his bedrooms was in fact a dining room and had been for many years so a Council Officer was despatched to view the room but because Dad is known to be volatile two of them showed up.

Dad is the least racist person you would ever meet and he said to them both "take a seat, would anyone like a drink"? He informed them that wherever they sat there was likelihood they would acquire dog hairs. The Muslim Housing Officer possibly showing off to the female Housing Officer began to talk down to Dad and attempted to embarrass him by demanding to know did I expect him to believe that I took food from the kitchen and then took it upstairs. Whoa! I covered my eyes because this was not going to be pretty "Get the fuck out of my home" Dad insisted and added "Who the fuck do you think you are"? Dad informed him that he had probably lived in his home longer than he had worked for the Council as he kept pushing him down the stairs with his hand in the small of his back. "Get out" he barked over and over again "how proud your parents must be of you". As I stated Dad is no racist and as always got on with everyone but his man's attitude was not very good. He was very much put in his place, Dad apologised to the lady for his language and told the man to never knock his door again or if he did he would face the consequences. If he was a little in doubt as to what that might mean I was tempted to get the machete from the back of the radiator and drop it at his feet.

Then all of a sudden the nasty mail came about me, like I am the biggest problem Nuneaton Council has got. It gave us an indication that choose whatever Dad and me were expected to downsize to a one bed roomed property and the only area that had the smaller properties were infested with heroin dealers and users and for sure Dad would end up back in jail amongst them low life scum because the machete would end up working overtime.

My Dad is old and I certainly am and he has lived here for twenty years and I had lived here for ten. What they were doing to him amounted to bullying and harassment, you can only prod a man for so long with a big stick. Especially if that man is my Dad, you will open up the biggest can of worms ever.

Somewhere along the way someone saw sense and gave Dad HISTORICAL PERMISSION for me to be able to live in the flats. We would have never left anyway I would have been up on the roof pouring boiling oil on anyone who tried to force entry. The forms Dad had to sign accepted me as a resident but he is not allowed to have a pet again after my demise, the horrible nasty people who just make the rules up as they go along. So if in the worst scenario I was to pass tomorrow this Council would expect my Dad to sit alone in a flat with the added comfort of a pet not allowed; Shame on You.

Should the rules change and he were allowed to have another pet the likely candidate would need to be seriously desert trained and aware of what he/she was about to face.

On this one particular day I had seen him in the kitchen with the bucket in the sink and it was getting filled with bleach, oven cleaner, Cillit Bang, Big Bad Dom, Bazooka that Varruca and just about everything was going into this mixture and he was stirring it with the wooden spoon (the same one that he stirred stews and curries with) and how it never blew up was beyond me. I could hear all the contents hissing like a snake and whatever he was cleaning was in for a big surprise. What I didn't realise and I'd forgot was he had caught me the previous evening having a scratch at the back of my ear. I froze when he went to pick me up OMFG it was me that was about to get blitzed and for the sake of perhaps ONE flea. Beforehand as a sort of starter, I was squirted at the back of my neck with some FRONTLINE flea treatment. However, that's not enough for this daft twat and his obsession with cleanliness, because no sooner had he put the FRONTLINE treatment on then he sat me in the sink and simply poured the contents of the bucket over me.

I couldn't breathe with the fumes and I imagined this is what the legal highs were like. My eyes would not stop rolling and I was properly spaced out but on the plus side that one flea would never hop, even once, ever again. He sat me on the settee and I couldn't focus for the life of me and I know how he felt like a one armed bandit on the settee with his own medication. But it was for a single flea, it's not like an army of them. Its all well and good living in this home but you daren't be seen scratching too often or you will be fumigated along with everything in the flat.

It would be fine if I was allowed to do the same to him because I hoped he had saved some of the contents of the bucket because when he had brought some girl home recently. I had seen her scratch now and again in her lower area and since then I had seen dearest Daddy raking in that same area with his house keys. The itch must have been that intense and I would much rather have my one flea than the army of irritants that are going to get under his skin in the not too distant future. How dare he be so concerned about my personal hygiene when his own was about to explode, literally in his lower region. It would be like an army of ants climbing over him and settling down and making it their home. Even Bazooka that Varruca will not shift this lot. If I've guessed right he will need to pour petrol on them to loosen their grip. It's at times like this its fucking fortunate he HAS stopped smoking because knowing his luck he would ignite the whole area; whilst he smoked and would blow his already tiny todger into oblivion.

Any new pet or even human lodger would need to take all of this into account before moving in. The man will test your patience to its furthest extreme. Living here is only for the head strong.

I've witnessed things you'd never believe possible and he will just stare at you the following day with his with his blank expression on his face that just says WHAT?

To him everything is quite normal but I've had ten years of it and I'm ready to retire and I want a sight more than a fucking carriage clock for what I've witnessed. I'm only a miniature dog and this fool has traumatised me. I deserve a medal and the least I'd accept is a George medal or Victoria Cross. You can shove the carriage clock up your arse OR up his which leads me into the next chapter.

CHAPTER NINE

In my first book ITS A DOGS LIFE you will recall a story of "Silly Bollox" placing me in the bath and shoving his fingers up my rectum, supposedly to unblock my anal glands. It was the most embarrassing moment of my life but Karma becomes a bitch when I tell you that Poppa G (my Father) has had several moments recently with fingers up his own anal area.

Sit down and make yourself comfortable and I will tell you all about it. The one person who wouldn't be able to sit comfortably is "Silly Bollox". It began with all of the recent problems regarding the weak bladder situation and he had been to see his Doctor at the Surgery. Bastard! Bastard! Bastard! It's one of the few places I'm not allowed in and I have to sit outside and wait patiently but I already knew because I had Googled his symptoms and no way would he be leaving that G.P.s room until he had been given a minimum of three fingers up his arse and possibly the whole fist (hopefully).   I ran around to the back of the Surgery and stacked some crates up by the window but I had chosen the wrong window   and although it was an old shrivelled up prune body I knew it wasn't his because I had seen him stripped off recently. As the semi naked body, turned around to get dressed I began to lose my balance on the crates and tipple over. Seeing what I can only describe as the weather beaten face of an old female buzzard was the final straw and the fall began towards the floor but I rolled better than any paratrooper   and regained my poise and scarpered around the corner before anyone realised about any of my voyeur activities.

I was sat all innocent when he came out and it did not matter where we went be it the pub, the park or just the town centre he never once wanted to sit down and he looked quite delicate. Oooh yes, you little beauty! He had been violated for sure and now maybe had a small inkling of what I went through. It is not nice is it, having fingers up and more music to my ears was listening to him tell his friend down the phone that it needed doing AGAIN! A second opinion was required L.O.L. God Bless, second opinions I tittered away to myself. No way was I missing this and the George Eliot Hospital in Nuneaton wasn't exactly a fortress. I got details from his letter and on the day of the appointment I made my way up to the Hospital, half an hour before and inched my way from corridor to corridor. Then I suddenly spotted the queue that stood out like a beacon with perhaps thirty nervous men all fidgeting and looking to the floor I hid under some chairs in the waiting room and watched as the men were being taken two at a time and I remember thinking "Jesus this Doctor loves doing two at a time". As they went through the door I slid through on the shiny polished floor and almost crashed into the far wall, the floor was that slippery. I got myself hidden beneath one of the beds and did not wish to see what was going off. Until Dad came in and by now I had realised that there were two Doctors in fact doing the examinations and it was like a production line of gloves, lube bin and then repeat and this probably went on every Saturday morning, finger blasting all the males with erectile problems. I sprang to attention when I heard the voice of "Silly Bollox" stating how many cigarettes he did or did not smoke and all of the usual jargon your get from them. I popped my head out for a clearer view and after they had exchanged pleasantries Dad was asked to bend over a chair and whoosh..... in the blink of an eye the Doctor was lubed up and inside Dads anus right up to the last knuckle. I gasped to stifle my laughter, this was golden, this was payback for my own intrusive insertion. Again I regretted not having brought a phone capable of capturing the moment because I would have blasted that all over Social Media. I made my way out of the room when the opportunity arose and made my own way to the canal tow path because I know that's the way he would come home and I pretended to just bump into him while I was having a stroll myself.

He spoke to me but he was certainly grumbling and muttering to himself, deeply upset at the morning's activities and apparently he had been told to report to his Doctors Surgery the following week for the results. When he did do even I would have hit the roof but having said that I still found it hilarious because he sat down and the Doctor opened the Hospitals brown envelope with the results and asked Dad to get up on the bed and roll over on to his side initially he thought it was perfectly innocent until whoosh... it happened again. Fingers in and fiddle about. Dad jumped up and said WTF I'm only here for results and that's the third time in a week I've been breached in the anal area. He demanded to know had they all been videoing it and was there now a video on the dark web called DAVE G TAKES IT LARGE.

He couldn't catch his breath and still nobody knew what was wrong with him. He did make it clear though that he definitely didn't want any more foreplay. He was sent back to the Hospital for further tests and was told he would need to have a camera down his pipe as in his Jap's eye and even the mention of it made his eyes water but a friend tried to allay his fears and told him it was painless. Upon attending the Hospital and seeing a Nurse at BOTH sides of the bed needing to hold an arm each, told him a very different story and no way would this be pain free and it was likely to be a few weeks before he was dancing the Macarena again.

He said he arched his back and spun his head around like the girl in the exorcist. His screams could be heard at the Hospital and in the next town. The pain was excruciating and his phone had kept ringing in his cat and the Nurse had said "Someone is popular" and I said it's my lift probably although I knew I didn't have one. On completion and sitting up Dad pretended a text message said his lift had arrived at the entrance. That was the only reason she agreed to let him go and he made a point of saying to then "well I don't know what all the fuss was about". Full of recently acquired bravado and waved them all goodbye.

He walked perhaps thirty steps down the corridor, fond the Public Toilet, laid on the floor and bit the paper towels and about cried a river L.O.L. After half an hour he tried to compose himself a little and finally left the cubicle and ventured outside. He had under estimated the pain and thought he would be okay but it became clear he was in a lot of pain and did not have a lift or any money for a taxi. I had laughed at the anal side of things but upon hearing the story to do with this latest appointment I felt guilty.

His friend Rafael Viola lives right by the Hospital and after a twenty minute walk, which would usually take five, he collapsed into one of Raff's armchairs and whimpered and whimpered with pain and was still the same when he got home. He couldn't make it up the stairs and kept dropping to his knees with a Lucozade bottle at the back of the settee and urinating into that whilst making noised that were blood curdling and upon checking the bottle there would have been hardly anything in it. The pain was like passing broken glass, he told his friend and he had been told, to drink LOTS of water to flush himself through but he knew that lots of water meant lots of urinating and in turn lots of pain so he kept any drinking to a minimum.

He still suffers with the same problem but refused to go to any Hospital and especially where lots of Doctors are lined up with disposable blue gloves o and a tube of lube in every fucking pocket ha-ha. Finger blasting on the NHS hey! Perhaps it wouldn't be so bad if they chucked a female Nurse into the mix now and again but knowing Dads luck he would end up with Hattie Jacques in Carry on Matron.

He did get sent a brown envelope and apparently he had to defecate in that and pop it back in the post and await the results. He kept thinking with his bad eyesight he would squat in the kitchen BUT miss the envelope time after time and there would be turds all over the kitchen floor. He thought it was the funniest thing ever that postmen and even sorting offices have to handle packages with turds in. Now that's what I would call Junk Mail. Jesus what a job! Dad never got around to doing it anyway and what will be, will be I suppose. We are both old and both going blind but not that blind that we wouldn't see some Doctor or Vet approaching us. I think we both had enough of that game and put NO ENTRY signs up in that area.

When I was peeping from under the bed at the Hospital I could have sworn one of the Doctors had a gimp mask on and both of them kept high fiving each other. This is what they mean by the NHS getting run down because they obviously can't get the Staff. Even all the cute Nurses walking by have little giggles to themselves because they know what the queue is for. He swears he will never go again and I've no reason to doubt him.

It wasn't until a few days later that he realised, that while he was laid in the Hospital toilet, he had taken a few of his dentures out but had forgotten to pick them up, when he stumbled out of there; over the bridge by the motorway bent over like QUASIMODO in the Hunchback of

Notre Dame. Be warned it's pain, its REAL pain; don't let anyone kid you different.

Now he had a different problem. With the teeth missing from his mouth and the big gap left behind it was a toss up which area had the biggest hole now. His mouth with the hole or his arse with all the prodding and poking; it would keep him quiet while he was without his dentures.

He had his image to hold onto the daft twat and if no dentures were in he would keep his mouth shut. He had said someone smashed a snooker ball into his mouth when he lost them and I didn't care to be honest. I simply warned him to be careful if one of the Doctors spun him the OTHER way round while he was bent over the chair. LOL

CHAPTER TEN

Because "Silly Bollox" had done his prostate tests and wasn't very happy with all of the outcome he had made a snap decision that we should both go up to Dewsbury which was the place of his birth and the plan was for us both to have a little holiday so BOTH of our cases were packed this time instead of just his.

Dewsbury had been a Catholic strong hold when Dad was a child but recently had been given the nickname Islamabad due to the influx of Muslims. It was plain to see why as soon as we arrived at the Station, because the ticket collector was on his knees and praying to the East. Outside of the station the taxi drivers were doing the same and it seemed the whole town was on its knees. The two prostrate Doctors back in Nuneaton would have a field day up here with everyone bent over. I soon realised that I couldn't get a taxi to my destination because of all of them praying and I didn't have too far to travel up to my friends so I decided to play leap frog all the way up there over their bodies knelt down.

Not a lot had changed, except the beards on the Muslims had got greyer and longer and they had multiplied tenfold. No shyness here, everyone must have been at it like rabbits. Dewsbury has changed quite a bit and heroin seems to have a stronghold on the whole area. Dad certainly knows, it's got a grip of his Son who he refuses to talk to and his Son believes Dad should love him no matter what but it's not going to happen. It hurts him when we go up there and we don't see him but why should we go up there for a break and become involved in drama.

We would always stop with our mate Mick Fox, his little dog Diva and his friend Lisa Marie would come around with her dog, so it would be a reunion for all of us. The adults and the dogs but if they went out I would boss the TV and the remote. All of the dogs knew I was a feisty little bitch and would give me a wide berth because I'd had fights up there before on previous visits and they knew that as small as I was, I was very much a handful.

It's nice up there with plenty of good long dog walks. While I was in the area without Dad knowing I popped down to the Catholic Church, St Paulinus and I went to see Father Hinchcliffe. He suggested I was a good girl that I could maybe became a Nun so I tried a few outfits on while I was there and the Priest blessed me and said I look just the part. He told me to learn all of the Stations the Cross and gave me some special Rosary beads and told me to pray for every sinner I knew. He had to be kidding on that one surely as it would take me forever and a day. By the time I left his company, I felt pure and chaste and decided to cleanse sinners, one day at a time and to begin at home first, where it should make things a little easier.

When I got back to Mick's they were all out at the pub. Dad had lots of friends up there who would all show up to have a drink with him. All of the usual suspects Lee Cass, Caron Morton, Kayle Asquith, Paula Bennett (Lady P) and many more I just can't remember off the top of my head. This is because I'm feeling all blessed, holy and have the urge to do Gods work.

No better place to start than Dads suitcase and my instincts proved right when I found sachets of drugs in his jeans, possibly, cocaine but it mattered little or nothing what if I said a few Hail Marys? Then tipped the powder straight down the toilet and left it floating on the surface for all of the sinners to see when they returned. I was sure they would understand and perhaps fall to their knees with me and say a quick prayer with me. Dad would take it well I was sure even though I calculated I had thrown £200 worth into the toilet. I couldn't wait to tell him and see the "delight" on his face as he realised he had no drugs for the weekend.|

I put my Nuns Habit and Rosary Beads into my case and went downstairs and waited for them all to come in from the pub. I had decided I would tell Dad about me becoming a Nun in the morning when we were alone; because nobody else knew I could talk and I'm sure even Dad didn't believe it and thought I was one of "The Others". He had become that accustomed to talking to himself or imaginary people that adding a little dog to the list shouldn't create a problem.

When they arrived back from the pub and with company Dad declared he had some party treats for everyone but within minutes of him getting upstairs, his voice boomed with my name and all of a sudden the earlier disposal did not seem like such a good idea at all. I was shouted for a very stern lecture and thought it wise to just take the lecture and not try to explain. By now everyone had left because of all the shouting and even Mick said he was going to have an early night. It seemed the best decision for me was to stay on the settee and let the dust settle and hopefully we would be fine in the morning; it was like being an old married couple.

In the morning I dressed in my Nuns Habit and waited for him to get up and I said a few prayers with my Rosary Beads and felt that once Dad saw how pure and chaste I looked he may be much more forgiving. To lighten his mood even more I decided to go and get a few breakfast provisions from the local shop and wrote down on a scrap of paper what I required.

Many of the shops in Yorkshire are little corner premises, exactly as you see in OPEN ALL HOURS on the TV with Arkwright in the corner shop, with lots of odds and ends on all the shelves but actually nothing you really needed. To make it much more complex as well these shops have been taken over by the Muslim Community and Mick's local shop was no different. It was now owned by MISTER BROWN and typical of any of these shops once you enter them you will discover about six people all stood about and just shaking hands and gossiping. They do more talking than a couple of women chatting over a garden fence.

I had made my list out but had not thought it out very well, because I was going to surprise Mick and Dad with a few cans or Carling to wash their breakfast down with and I had also put bacon on the shopping list. I pushed the door open to the shop and as expected there stood a gang of chattering Muslims. They looked around for a while to see who had actually opened the door, before one looked down and nudged the others, pointed down and there was yours truly dressed in all of my Nuns attire. "Can I help you" Mr Brown said and I pushed the note towards him and he motioned to get the first two items on the list, these were eggs and bread. While all of the others spoke in their own tongue and laughed a lot and it was obvious I was a figure of fun. I didn't mind because the mood was jovial and I smiled at any of them who made eye contact. "Bastard" whoosh... I felt the wind from the sword as Mister Brown almost beheaded me and I thought it wise not to hang about for the rest of the order. I ran like the wind straight out of the door with the whole pack of them in pursuit, I knew how the fox felt being pursued by the hounds. "Bastard" he shouted "you little bastard" and other Muslims came running out of some of the homes and I didn't dare look around at how many were chasing me.

I was in fear for my life but out of the corner of my eye I recognised one of the streets as being where one of Dads good friends lived. Katherine Fallas had looked after Dad in the past and given him a home when he needed one and he would always thank her for that. BUT right now I needed a home much more than he ever did, so I hurdled, her garden gate and hid myself in one of her bushes in the garden. "Allah Akbar" I could hear a few of them shouting and screaming and although I didn't know what it actually meant; I definitely knew they weren't saying "Your order is ready to pick up". Kath's door opened and I ran in gratefully and although she had a Staffordshire bull terrier, I had met him before and we both got on; so after I had gathered my breath we all had a good laugh at the situation.

I now understood though why the area had been re-named Islamabad. It was madness and Kath said to me that I would be okay anytime now because it was morning prayers. We all peeped through the curtains until eventually the baying mob just all dropped to the floor and began rambling and praying. This was my opportunity and after Kath telling me to give her love to my Dad I scampered out of the door and even went through one of my very complex gymnastic routines and done a handspring over Kath's gate and began to leap frog over all the knelt bodies.

Wisely, I now had my Nuns habit in a carrier bag and as I stood on the back of one of the praying Muslims; I waved to Kath with the sword that I had now claimed for my own. I had made good my escape through all the back gardens on the Estate but little knowing that in every single garden on the way through, I had sliced through every single washing line which would not go down too well with Mick's neighbours.

I hadn't had a good start to the morning at all and I was not looking forward to another lecture from Dad so I pretended to be asleep on the settee when they had both got out of bed.

Diva, Mick's dog wanted to know where I had been but I just put a finger to my lips to indicate it was best she didn't know. I had already begun to have my doubts at taking my vows and becoming a Nun. When that decision was taken out of my hands with a text message from Father Hinchcliffe, stating they had discovered I had a love child called Millie. Who lived with a friend of Dads, Adam Green who was a well respected local businessman in Nuneaton? It would perhaps be better if we kept all of this scandal a little bit low key for all concerned. So I took the decision to forget about becoming a Nun. As I did not want to bring any disruption to Millie's life as I certainly loved her and I had heard that she had recently had pups and I was now a Grandma. I would need to wet

the puppies' heads I suppose BUT definitely not
from MISTER BROWN's shop L.O.L.

CHAPTER ELEVEN

When they both got up Mick shouted to Dad "there's a can in the fridge if you want one Dave" and added that he was going to make some bacon and egg sandwiches. "Fucking, fantastic" I cursed myself for not having checked the fridge earlier BUT on the plus side I had come away intact because I dread to think what would have happened if Kath hadn't have saved me.

I hoped we were going home soon, because I didn't fancy pushing my luck by being in the area to long now, in case there was wanted posters stuck up all round the Estate. I had nightmare visions of me being some sort of sacrificial offering to Allah and no way would I be able to fight all of them off with just the scimitar I had stolen from them. That would certainly come in handy though, next time I went to stay in Dawlish beach with Dads friend Neil Salter and I could fight the seagulls off with it. When I had been to Dawlish before I was certain the seagulls were working as a team and trying between them to wear me out fighting them off until I had become weary and one of them could perhaps lift me and carry me to some hilltop to eat me alive between them. I imagined me dropping to one knee and slicing them all in half, like Indiana Jones would, with the very finely honed weapon.

Dad was going to visit a few of his friends before he left Yorkshire and because I did not want to go he teased me about being jealous because it was mainly females, he was going to visit Tracy Quinn, Theresa Hall, Angela Walshaw and all of the Morton girls but I did not want to venture out, in case I was recognised. That was the only reason I declined a day out. I definitely would not have been flavour of the month upon stepping out of the front door. Also if any of the local neighbours had an inkling that they needed to do yet another days washing because of me then they may peg me out on the line instead and take it in turns shoving a dirty mop in my face for the rest of the day. No Sir, a day out was the last thing I needed; once they had left I made myself a drink, got a packet of dog treats and planned on a lazy day on Mick's sofa.

I grabbed Mick's laptop and caught up on any notifications that I had missed. I was certainly a much busier dog nowadays, since I had written my first book and had it published on Amazon. Once I had dealt with my all of my book sale transactions I decided to have a sneaky little look on Dads pages. I had long since worked out his passwords to access some of his sites and oh my, what an eye opener. He had been a very busy little boy with his search engine and I was shocked when I saw the two words X HAMSTER because rather foolishly I thought he was getting another pet until my eyes could not believe what I was seeing and very red faced I had to look away although admittedly, I had to cast my eyes back to try and work out just how a human body could be that flexible L.O.L.

I checked out a few things to do with this own book sales as well because his first book WELLIES AND WARDERS. Which was still earning him Royalties each month from Amazon after it was first published four years previously, it had actually sold in fourteen countries and had became a number one best seller forty-eight hours after it release; it had staggered him at the time albeit in a nice way, that was.

Everything was back on track and up to date and I should have left it at that but curiosity got the better of me and I started to have a little spy on his Messenger. I don't usually get jealous but the name Anna Tink Guziejewska came up quite a lot and when I looked she was a very pretty Polish girl he met while he was out in Torremolinos in Spain. After reading many of the exchanges it soon became clear Anna wasn't a threat and was just some lovely natured girl Dad had met while drunk outside some Irish Bar. He seemed to spend a lot of time in Spain didn't he, but it will come as no surprise to discover that even this holiday became yet another ill fated jaunt. I remembered him going and the firm promise he made to himself that he was going to have a good relaxing holiday and give drugs a wide berth and have himself a little Rehab. His Rehab, if you could call it that, lasted a matter of hours because he bumped into two Russian criminals. Who seeing my Dads tattoos and it seeming obvious that he had been in prison the conversation turned to English Jails and Russian Jails. They all had a good laugh and at one stage one of the Russians put his finger under his nose and said in broken English "hey my friend, do you like" and it were clear what he was asking, did I like or not and once the seed is planted in "Silly Bollox" head there is no refusing and they had spent the rest of the evening at some mad Moroccans flat; sniffing what turned out to be very good quality cocaine and Dad said his whole face was numb.

I loved Dad and I wished he didn't do it at all but I had long since accepted that his life had been difficult ad this was his only way of dealing with it. He didn't feel answerable to anyone to be honest; if anyone was offended he did not really care because HIS life belonged to HIM to lead and was not for others to dictate to him that it was wrong. In my opinion he had very much cut down on his intake since I had first come to live with him. His whole life had been the same and he had always dabbled in drugs either selling or using and it had just become natural and a way of life.

He got voted the Speaker of the Year at the Women's Institute in Nuneaton and the main reason for this is because he would always speak THE TRUTH and that's the only way to be in life. It would be pointless him standing there and telling out and out lies if he was asked a question. He could see one or two were visibly shocked though at some of his revelations, Caz Price and Susan Williamson who ran the organisation could be seen covering their eyes and probably thinking "OMG what did he just say" L.O.L. But that's my Dad in a nutshell and he is talking about the person HE HAD BEEN, in contrast to the person he was now.

He never pretends to have been no Saint in his formative years but he certainly feels he has turned all of that around now and was even recently voted Outstanding Member of his Community so in a way he must be doing something right. If he hits the bottle now and again or binges on drugs, obviously, there is a reason behind all of that and it's either comfort for him OR it's a release and makes him open up and talk.

All of us are surrounded by a multitude of so called pillars of society who will lie, connive and deny any wrong in their lives and it's a complete tissue of lies and when I listen to him criticising them, then for sure he is right. He always says "hey Stella I can look in my mirror and be happy" and I get what he says all day long; because he feeds everyone when he can ill afford to do so. If he knows anyone at all in a prison he will send them stamps and writing materials; even if the cost of it of it means he cannot afford bread or milk because his view is that he can get his essentials borrowed from one of his neighbours whereby a prisoner cannot. He knows because he has spent eleven years in different institutions so he realised the importance of something as simple as a stamp. He doesn't ever let anybody down and if he wants to take drugs to ease his own burden, then that's nobody's business but his own and the one thing he never does is hide the fact. He is a very truthful person!

Anyway, I pissed myself to learn that two hours into his so called Rehab he was off his head with two Russians who had Kalashnikovs tattooed on their chests and faces. It would have taken anybody else weeks or months to find two nutcases like this pair but he had done it within a few hours of landing from Alicante. It seemed that every time he flew abroad he would find himself with drama and especially in Spain. The Gods smiled on him, I suppose ad he led a charmed life because he could have ended up in one of the Spanish prisons, quite a few times and God know what I would have done if he had been locked up over there on remand for months.

When the Lucky Lucky Men had been knocked out in Tenerife he thought that was really funny but I didn't even raise a smile, I was that angry. I had noted in his Messenger that he was making arrangements to go out and stay with his friend Ski, out in Spain; this pair wouldn't be the best combination to get together as drama seemed to follow them. Anthony laan Hart (Ski's name), was very much a legendary figure and he had recently taken the decision to move out to live in Spain and got himself a home with a swimming pool; that would put even the Love Island baste to shame. Ski had been a cage fighter when he lived in the United Kingdom and was a very nice natured lad. He would always be at the front of the queue if Dad needed any help raising money for the charity Doorway, which was responsible for the care and well being of the local teenagers in the area who were homeless. He had slept rough overnight with Dad, to raise much needed funds for them and I was so glad this move seemed to have worked out for Ski.

Antoniohartio is an Instagram sensation with all of his lifestyle out there and it couldn't have happened to a nicer person and he took my mate out there with him. His own little dog called Shakira (I kid you not). I'd love to go out with Dad if only to make sure I kept them both out of trouble, which would be no mean task. All the good life has made Ski put on a bit of timber and there's no denying it because in the words of Shakira THE HIPS DON'T LIE L.O.L. This lad could win any reality show because he would get a large chunk of the gay vote as well because he would be their idea of the perfect pin up poster boy. It's a recipe for disaster if Ski and Dad get together but reading these messages exchanged between them then it's a racing certainty that they will be causing problems in one of the Spanish bars very shortly. I had to admit it did look a good life out there and quite peaceful until Ski had gone out there to live and riding his scrambler bike off the cliff and straight into the sea.... while still sat on it. He never does things in half measures and as all the broken bones to prove it; if you chose to spend time with him then you certainly put your very life into his hands.

I gradually became tired and had myself an afternoon nap and waited for Dad to come home because we would be packing later that evening and going back to Nuneaton in the morning. I had closed the laptop and put it away. I read Dads stuff often but he wouldn't have a clue with mine or could to get in because he would never guess the password. It was "Sillybolloxhammers19" which I will explain in the next chapter.

CHAPTER TWELVE

It was certainly an endurance test living with "Silly Bollox" and when we had got home, I just placed the sword/machete on the top of the unit in the living room where it would just blend in with the rest of the armoury.

By now I'd guess that he had completely lost count of the weapons around him but for sure no matter which room of the house he was in he would know where to lay his hands on one within seconds. What was it though with Yorkshire men and hammers because I kid you not there were four different ones throughout the flat. One on top of the fridge, by the front door, in the kitchen, one on the bathroom and one at the side of BOTH of the beds on the bedside tables.

One by his bed and strangely in my opinion, one at the side of the bed in the guest room; God knows what any guests unpacking felt about it. However, if they were staying overnight they would be obviously aware of Dads quirky ways.

From another angle Dad did have a friend who had been shot twice in the head and murdered; one of the neighbours along with his wife had been arrested as the Police had discovered an UZI sub machine gun and a thousand rounds of ammunition. All of this was in the flat NEXT DOOR and it certainly did not make for a good night's sleep; especially for a man suffering with anxiety and depression and if he was nervous if rubbed off on me because obviously I was meant to be the guard dog of the premises. Don't get me wrong because I was primed and alert at all times and constantly watching the front door BUT that was to go in the opposite direction if anyone came through the door. Somehow or other I did not think that one or more hammers would be a match would be a match for gun toting ; to be on the safe side I had adopted Dads stew pot to be my place of safety and I would come out when I thought it was all over should anything ever happened. The stew pot would often feed more people than Jesus did in the desert with five loaves and two fishes. It was very wide and deep and if I curled myself up into a cosy little ball and crawled inside it and then flipped it over it would be perfect fit and my own personal sort of air raid shelter.

The area really was that mad and another neighbour had hung himself with grenades strapped to him while he was dressed in his favourite camouflage outfit. The man would always be up trees in the local park and observing everyone with his field binoculars. When he finally flipped and pulled the pins at the same time he hung himself he was obviously planning on taking other people with him but

135

fortunately for the other residents they were duds that had been disarmed.

While I had always thought "Silly Bollox" was a complete nutcase it gave me an indication that here were much more seriously deranged people out there than him. The area we lived in just seemed to be a hot bed of violence and many incidents of violence and to be on the safe side maybe Dad should walk about with a stew pan on his head. With everyone being aware of how strange Dads behaviour could be nobody would have actually batted an eyelid to see him walking around the Estate with a very big stew pan on his head with the handle at the front like a dalek and pulling another pan alongside him with yours truly tucked up inside it. These are the sorts of neighbourhoods that Sun Life post their insurance plans through the door TWICE a day, the threat of violence is that rife.

As the Police had discovered a cache of arms in the flats, if they ever needed to attend the flats they would do so in great numbers. Even if it was only a minor incident, for a period of time the whole Estate would be on lock down and anyone coming or going would be monitored including nutcases with saucepans on the their head L.O.L. This was the atmosphere we would live in on a daily basis and what led to the introduction of building dens at the back of the settee; where Dad lived for days at a time. I would need to pick my food bowl up and drop it by him for remind him that I needed feeding and at these times he would look shocked that I had even found him because he felt his hideaway was impenetrable.

Days and days I would need to live with Dave Doolittle like, this while he talked away to himself rather than the animals. When he lived in a paranoid state all the times he had and imagining Police around every corner, to be suddenly in a situation where there is ACTUALLY Police around every corner; it doesn't bear thinking about and especially when the Police are even knocking at the door and shouting "hello, hello, hello" through the letterbox. Trust me it's a paranoid schizophrenics worst possible nightmare and he had retreated into his den and doubled up on his medication.

Hand guns had now been found at the local pub which was only a hundred yards away and it had become that scary for the local constabulary; that I imagined one or two of the weaker kneed ones would rather be in the den with me and Dad. I thought I had better order more saucepans from Amazon.

There always seemed to be violence hanging in the air and a little down the line, a few years later, nothing much had changed and we had already had a few bad tragedies in the town due to incidents of stabbings and with it being a small town we not only knew the perpetrators but we also knew the victims and their families. We couldn't sympathise enough and obviously felt their loss.

When we thought things couldn't get any worse the enormity of the affect of knife crime hit home and brought our whole family the biggest nightmare we could ever possibly imagine. My brother, Glenn's son Bradd was stabbed to death in the street in front of his father. None of us will ever recover from that day and we have constant reminders of that fateful day when each time we turn on the news on the TV and there is a story of another death by stabbing, it drives it home. Especially for Bradd's widow Harriet, who is a beautiful girl and person, who is now tasked with bringing up their three small children singlehandedly. We have every confidence in her because she is an exceptional Mother to the children, Mickey who is eight, Romi who is seven and little Jaxx who is four and all of us as a family will be there to support her throughput this journey. God Bless Harriet and also their three small children; RIP Bradd you will be sadly missed.

It is at times like this when it is plain to see the calibre of people around you and my friend from his maximum security cell Charlie Bronson Salvador would send his friend Rod Harrison to Bradd's funeral with a wreath for Bradd and the Family. Also I had asked Charlie to send my brother a little message of support to raise his spirits and he did that without hesitation and even took his support to a different level for me, my Dad and all of the Family. Charlie is part of our Family now and none of us will ever stop showing and giving him support. How can a man be held for forty – four years when is has not killed or raped anybody? None of us really care that he took a terrorist hostage, bundled him under his bed and barricaded himself in. The twat was a terrorist who brought terror to the streets of the United Kingdom. I have no sympathy with a person such as this and Dad and many others would all feel the same. All of Charlies transgressions are historical events and Charlie has been no trouble for many years now and all of the Media choose to report on Charlie's past misdemeanours over and over because they have no intention of reporting him in a favourable light. I can state here and now, I have watched all of the help, he has given Dad to raise much needed funds for at least a dozen charities in Nuneaton and for a few organisations up in Yorkshire, my place of birth.

Moreover at this moment in time he has initiated action in encouraging young people to put down their knives and save lives. Many boxing promoters and other people have been taking this message to the youngsters and speaking to them, showing them Bradd's story with photos of him and his children and if that don't bring the message home than nothing will.

If it saves even one life then it has been worthwhile. I find it strange how the Media decide not to pick up on the positive things Charlie does from the seclusion of his cell and accept he is no longer the person who the wish him to be. My Dad will never say one bad word about him or Rod or many of the other good people he had met through the campaign for the release of Charlie. It will happen and then one day he can come round here and we will all have a game of scrabble with pans on our heads. God bless you Charlie your day will come.

Dad showed me where you hide a mouse on all of your art work, which he has got on his wall and I think it's time a little Jack Russell was hid in one of them. You are a good man Charlie Bronson Salvador and Nuneaton loves you pal. Dad laughs that you pair are just as nuts as each other and that you are both about the same age; how ironic is it that your are from Luton and he is from Dewsbury, which are both the most Muslim strongholds in the country. How many similarities have you pair got between you? I think this daft twat still wishes he was in solitary and that's why he keeps retreating into his den.

The Justice Department have got a lot to answer for regarding his many mental health issues because they have certainly contributed to that. He is on about eight different lots of medication now and his away and bouncing off the walls most days, but it's all good fun and I just tap dance on the coffee table until it has a calming effect on him.

On behalf of all of the Family I would like to thank you so much for the contribution you have made towards easing all of our grief a little, especially with your ongoing campaign, which goes a long way towards keeping Bradd's memory alive whenever random strangers hear his story.

It is a strange and violent world we are all living in now and Dad prefers going for a drink during the day rather than be outdoors on a night, when many of the youngsters have little or no respect for anyone. You and my Dad are old school Charlie and he worries for you coming out here amongst it. Everybody getting released from prison now should be issued with a bullet proof and stab proof vest, a discharge grant and a pan for your heads.

CHAPTER THIRTEEN

We were having yet another long walk down the canal but on this occasion it would have a dual purpose because the bank we used in our home town, Nuneaton, was closed for refurbishment and for the next few months we would need to for to the neighbouring town of Bedworth; going down the canal exercised me also with the six mile return journey.

I would never be on the lead and had myself many a good fight with the bigger dogs on the canal tow path and I would strut about like the Lion King. I would fear no dog, the bigger the better because if I sank my teeth into that lower carriage while I was underneath there, it would definitely bring a tear to their eye and I would soon be declared the winner.

Whilst approaching Bedworth Dad saw a girl who used to live in our flats, Lorraine Hardy and her friend Kay Downs both walking dogs; Dad would always be flirting with Kay if he saw her, so I made a point of nipping that in the bud straight away, as I attacked both of their dogs and they all screamed and scattered and picked their dogs up and cursing me but I found it quite amusing as they all scampered away.   Dad couldn't take his eyes away from Kay with her tight denim shorts, "nothing wrong with your eyes now, you old bastard is there" I said while all the time teasing him.

It was a very hot summer's day and after he had done his banking we sat outside Witherspoon's pub in the town centre. Dad went in and ordered a pint and a breakfast, after he paid for it he asked for a bowl of water for me

146

and all hell broke loose "oh we didn't know you had a dog or we wouldn't have served you" they stated. Dad was already sat OUTSIDE with his beer and after a very heated argument he told them to go away and he would leave after he had ate his breakfast. God Bless to the lady who ran the cafe next door because she brought me some water out; that I lapped up gratefully. While Dad was getting it explained to him that there was now a blanket ban on dogs inside or outside any of their pubs and apologised. I don't know if they expected this information to appease Dad in any way because all he kept saying over and over again, several times was FUCK OFF, in a very loud voice and for them to move away while he ate. I could plainly see him getting a little angry, I knew all of the signs with Daddy dearest and after he had ate half of the breakfast he put the plate on the floor for me to eat and declared "There's no rush Stella".. Although they were perhaps a little reviled at me eating from the plate nobody attempted to take the plate away from me. Apparently, it's a nationwide ban and just in the Weatherspoon Pubs and that has to be accepted I suppose. Though, it wouldn't have harmed anyone giving a dog a bowl of water. Then Dad wouldn't have needed to stop using this particular pub again by choice because he was now obviously banned as he threw his lager up the wall and didn't hang about to listen to the outcome L.O.L.

Knowing him like I did though he had a certainly let them off lightly because a few years prior to that he would have let his chair go through the window. I'm not saying that's the correct thing to do in anyway whatsoever ever but his brain reacts differently to ours. Any Psychiatrist who had treated him would give you the same diagnosis, that Dad was a danger to himself and certainly a danger to the public. His last shrink readily admitted that he felt unsafe sitting in the same room as him L.O.L. It is all well and good for them but I have to actually

LIVE with him and not just sit with him for half an hour or less if they could get away with it.

We had had enough of Bedworth and its pettiness and set off back down the canal. There's never a problem with me being in the water, if I've got the big extendable lead on so that I can swim freely but should he need to pull me out he can do so whenever he likes which is his safety net because I go completely deaf once I hit the water.

He has two key words though and I never need inviting twice and if I hear them two words "GET IN", then I am like an Olympic swimmer as I dive in. We are walking along the path and Dad is still angry at recent events. His phone rings and it's his friend that wants to inform him he has just won the Irish lottery for the second time in a week, several thousand pounds was waiting to be collected and Dad shouted excitedly "GET IN" to his friend but unfortunately for Dad that was

149

my cue to become a leaping salmon and I hit the water with a big splash. I was swimming freely towards the outer bank and as much as Dad tried to coax me back towards him, I could hear nothing. Each time I saw his face he just appeared to be waving to me which he was but it was in panic.

He paced up and down, as I swam back and forth in the reeds and all of a sudden my confident manner took a knock, as I realised one of my paws was caught and wouldn't move and I began to flounder. Dad had noticed that I was struggling and also realised he had very little time to reach me, before I went under and although he can't swim, he had been in the water on other occasions and knew it wasn't very deep; albeit littered with lots of awkward rubbish on the canal bed.

This was why I loved Dad, as I watched him lower himself into the water until it was midway up his chest. He waded towards me and after a few stumbles he reached me, broke me free from the reeds and brambles that had wrapped round me. He turned just in time to see one of the many barges on the canal boring down on us, they hadn't even seen us, as he held me up over his shoulders and free from the water. The only thing missing was the theme music from Titanic except us pair were the iceberg L.O.L. The canal is a busy one to be honest and we would need to get back across to the inner bank before more traffic came.

After a few trips and scares we reached the bank and he deposited me on the tow path, but he could not clamber out himself because of the weight of the water on his clothes. He attempted to climb out a few times but he was struggling, so to raise attention I kept barking and barking until I saw some figures running towards us. It turned out to be people we knew from around Hilltop, as much as Dad was embarrassed because the incident would be the next few days' gossip it mattered little, because the important thing was we had got him out of the water. We thanked them and Dad took all of his wet clothes off and walked down the canal naked carrying them; with one or two people shouting, "has your Dad not taken his tablets Stella"? It was wise not to laugh because he had a face like thunder.

I would certainly cuddle up next to him that night because without playing down the incident, I would have gone under if he hadn't taken the risk to reach me. I couldn't praise him any higher because I knew his fear of water is extreme. Without a doubt he had saved my life; but the real tragedy was that people would gossip tomorrow about him being stuck in the water and about him being nude down the canal. Gossips and nasty mouthed people don't see the bigger picture.

At least Dad had begun to realise that not everyone who appears to be a friend, are actually what it says on the tin. He preferred drinking at home now, then he could relax more and I preferred it as well because it was just the pair of us. Rather than sitting amongst certain people he regarded as fake now. My Dad is a real kind man to everyone. Two close "friends" and a family member had even turned against him for whatever reason; he now calls them the Posh and Becks of Attleborough with their own little love child called Baron. It was funny now we were away from it all but we didn't need none of that and other peoples drama in our lives.

We had an off license straight across, a big park and canal and if the weather was good the bus pass was out. On them days Dad would always come back in a better mood because we had enjoyed ourselves. Drinking locally never done him many favours, because he is too kind natured and always dealing with everyone's problems. It wasn't like any of them bothered that he had problems of his own.

These people had shown their true colours and would not be welcome in our company again. Life becomes a learning curve I suppose, it soon becomes clear who plays games around you and who is genuine. I am sure that Dad enjoys what he sees in the mirror and especially now he had just saved my life. My hero, he makes my heart swell; very true story.

There was also a lesson to be taught about staying on the lead in future that could have assisted me in getting out of the water and any difficulty. I wouldn't fancy seeing the look on his face should he ever have to do the same thing again. As much as I was obsessed with water, I became hesitant about diving in the canal again for the next few months. It had been a very scary experience for me, as you would appreciate if you could see how small I am and with me knowing how scared Dad was of water. I envisioned the pair of us drowning, sinking to the bottom and nobody realising until weeks later. Then some young kids "scrapping" in the canal pulling Dad out of the water on the end of their magnets by all of the fillings in his mouth L.O.L.

The incident just strengthened the bond that we had always had and I would gladly walk by his ankle always looking up admiringly.   I would always protect him and I did not have to wait long to display my loyalty.

Dad had been having lots of trouble down the Benefits Office and continually being underpaid and because of his boisterous behaviour he had been asked to leave and when he had refused the Police had been sent for. Oh dear! Ouch! When many people thought this was them playing their ace card with "Silly Bollox", it would have the completely opposite effect. So I would find myself a wall to sit on with a comfortable view and let battle commence.

"Look Mr Ginnelly, the lady knows her job" the Officer declared! "How the fuck do you know she knows her job and is doing it correctly"? Stated Dad and pointed out to him he was only an inexperienced Community Constable. Shouting great come back Dad! However, it seemed the Community PC couldn't handle being embarrassed in front of people and grabbed Dad and placed him up the wall with his arm up his throat to stifle him from even speaking.

Stella to the rescue, because no way was anyone placing their hands on my Dad, I dived off the wall and raced across and sank my teeth firmly into his ankle. "You little bastard" he shouted and began to hop on his good leg but no way was I letting him out of jail yet, as I bit the good leg and tore his trouser leg as he fell over cursing me. He was reaching for his taser but me and Dad raced away through the park before reinforcements were dispatched. Once we had put a good distance between ourselves and the situation, we laughed and laughed and high fived each other till our wrists ached. Yes it was certainly funny but the reality was they knew Dads name from the Benefit Office; we would be seeing Robocop again of that I was certain.

CHAPTER FOURTEEN

Knowing how the Police overreacted around here, I wouldn't be surprised if my face was not planted on wanted posters on lampposts throughout the Estate. "Silly Bollox" was sleeping like a top, nothing new there the amount of Zopiclone he had taken, but I was nervous and on edge and kept going out on the landing and checking the car park for any Police activity.

When Dad used to grow cannabis I had made myself a chute/slide, out of the silver tubing he had used for ventilation. To ensure that I could just career down it, like the rubble comes down something similar on a building site and I would expect to land at the front of the flats with my feet running. While I was on sentry duties out on the landing, I noticed two men to do with the Council acting all guarded outside one of the flats down the landing. So I ambled along till I was close enough to hear the conversation between them, apparently it was not the first time they had attended this sort of situation in the flats. I was now very curious as to what had taken place but they made it clear for me to go away every time. I heard them talking about the need to break something up to get it through the door. Being the helpful dog I am, I rushed back to my own flat, made my way back to them and dropped two hammers by their feet and they repeated earlier demands for me to go away. No way could I let this go, I dragged the trampoline along the landing to where the two men blocked all access to the flat, I could see there were thousands of flies all hovering about behind them; as I began to gently bounce up and down, until I had a little momentum and was high enough to look over their shoulders. I saw a male figure with a bottle of whiskey still in his hand BUT in a state of rigor mortis, in the chair which was obviously the exact spot he had died. Now I understood the passing conversation, about breaking something up because they had meant the bones of the man to get him out of the door, as the Undertaker and Mortician would need to do the exact same to get the body in a coffin.

Ooosh! That sent a shiver down my spine and even though I understood the harsh realities of death; I would try not to mention this to "Silly Bollox", because he would have a field day. Whenever he went out into one of his anxious depressive spells, he would squeeze every last drop out of the doom and gloom content of a single person living in a flat.

As I bounced up and down on the trampoline one of the men motioned to swat some of the flies and I mistakenly thought he was trying to hit me and instinctively arched myself back until "ping"... I went out of the side, over the landing rails and hurtled towards the grass below. I had watched war films on the TV and knew how to do a roll, like a paratrooper, to cushion my fall although I still hurt my hip a little. While I became the centre of attention, with the other residents of the flats as a crowd had gathered around me. I looked up to see the very funny sight of the two men carrying the dead body, in the chair still, along the landing hastily. I was sure I had seen one of them swigging the whisky from the bottle and all of the flies followed like a swarm of locust. Not a pretty way to die and I hoped Dad hadn't seen it or heard them say they'd done it many times before as they passed our door or none of us would hear the last of it. Fortunately, he had seen me laid on the floor and had come running to see what had occurred. "Does Stella need an ambulance" someone asked and I laughed and thought no she doesn't but there's a man sat in a chair that needs a furniture removal van L.O.L.

Dad took me over to the P.D.S.A in Coventry, where I have always been looked after. I knew many of the other dogs in the waiting room as we had all grown up together, albeit living in different towns.

For a long time I had been getting away with it, when Dads friends at the pub would be teasing him, saying that I'd got a double chin or a spare tyre and he would forget about it as soon as he heard them. BUT he had always taken the Vets advice seriously and she had uttered those dreaded words. "We have checked Stella thoroughly Mr Ginnelly, she is fine and not in any pain but my Colleague and I both agree she is looking a little PODGY". Oh nooo! That's all he needed to hear and I would now be on one of the famous Atkins diets and would be rationed and on the bathroom scales six times a day. Every time I looked in my bowl for the next few days there would be a lettuce leaf, sliced tomatoes and celery. Chinese and Indian takeaways

162

would be off the menu for the foreseeable future and already my stomach rumbled and yearned for food. Someone on the landing mentioned they were sick of the flies still hovering about and I thought "well they aren't hovering about my bowl because there is fuck all in it". This was no way to live, I wanted to scream at him and say we were entitled to put on weight when we are older but none of it would have even registered with him anyway.

It had triggered a reaction in him and this time he was taking it a stage further and TWO Passports to Leisure dropped through the letterbox. I already had a vision of him wrapping me in a bin liner and making me walk mile upon mile on the treadmill while he bench pressed 20LBS the useless skinny little weakling. I would cringe watching him check his "muscles" out in one of the gym mirrors at the Pingles. I doubt he had ever been to a gym before and he was comical to watch flexing his arms. If anyone existed who was that puny he would get sand kicked in his face then it was "Silly Bollox". When we had left the gym one day and had a stroll into town he had become a little tired, he said and felt a little dizzy, so he got a cup of water from one of the shop keepers by the fountain. He sat down against the wall in the sun and the heat made him close his eyes and have forty winks. God knows how he must have looked, as a few people who passed by, threw lots of change into the cup and I had to laugh that we may have looked like beggars L.O.L. At this point I decided to put a show on for them, I began to walk on my front paws around the fountain and once people cheered it encouraged me more and I began to moonwalk backwards and forwards. The cup began to overflow with coins and I was singing I'm on Fire by Kasabian in my head. Not all people like giving beggars money and as if like a gift from God above, one of the audience threw me one of Greggs finest sausage rolls, I broke it into three sections. All of the crowd cheered and clapped, as I juggled all three pieces while

164

standing on a tennis ball with my free paw. All of the noise woke Dad up with a start, it was now time to add being a magician to my act, as one by one as the pieces of sausage roll fell and they fell straight into my accepting mouth and disappeared forever. "Fuck the Atkins diet" I thought and I devoured the tasty morsels and craved even more.

Word of warning to all of my friends in this town, all who know, love me and would never wish me harm. Please, please, please do not ever mention the word PODGY to him, when talking about me or you have practically signed my death warrant by starvation.

He looked amazed that he had £18.53 in his cup and I was going to suggest we both go and have a nice steak but I doubt he would have agreed to that so it was a case of saving my breath. He settled for plan B and that was a few pints for HIMSELF and a Chinese takeaway again for HIMSELF! To say I was a little peeved would be an understatement and if he thought I would be tap dancing my way around the fountain again he was mistaken.

I had been placed on a diet and I was a member of the local gym but even that wasn't enough for his daft twat because he had got me an application form to join Weight Watchers. I am a miniature Jack Russell FFS and if I lost anymore weight I could live in a matchbox in his pocket. I was glad in a way he had joined me up with Weight Watchers because questions would soon be asked when I was winning Slimmer of the Week EVERY FUCKING WEEK! "Put your glasses on now and again" I would shout at him when we were alone. He had pinned all my Diplomas up on my wall in my little retreat home under the stairs and I looked like a Japanese Prisoner of War while this daft twat was telling everybody proudly that "Stella had won another

award" L.O.L. I had to laugh or I would cry a
river with "Silly Bollox".

The one plus about it was that I had
laughed with others about the fact that any Police
looking for me, would struggle as I no longer
resembled that dog and would claim it was
mistaken identity and be absolved of all charges.
That didn't matter in the end because the Family
Solicitor Chris Pendle had been down to view the
CCTV, he had expressed concern about the
Officer putting his hands by Dads throat; rightly
so and the Inspector readily agreed so he case
was closed.

A funny incident followed not long after,
Dad received a letter from the DWP and he
misread the letter stating that he was being
investigated from 2014. Dad believed it was to
do with Royalties, which he had already
explained to them were a pittance. He began to
throw furniture about and I made myself scarce

and ran away out of the firing line. We visited lots of pubs that day and Dad was in a blind rage and was wondering why he always had to be plagued by bad luck. Later that day he came across his son Troy who lives in Tamworth, we all went back to the flat together. It must have looked as if we had been burgled by the state of the flat but Dad just indicated for Troy to read the DWP letter and that it would explain everything. Troy sat, read the letter and laughed at the fact Dad had sat with no electric the previous evening when all the time he had £2,300 in the bank. Yes, the DWP had been investigating Dad BUT only to work out what they owed HIM .

Was he the only man alive that could sit in darkness with no food and break his furniture up in a mood with the DWP, when they had actually deposited a healthy balance in his Bank?

Craziness and lunacy at its finest,
madness and mayhem the main features of Dads life. I would feel sorry for him at times though,

because where was the Community Constable now who threatened him with arrest and stated the decision was correct? Anyway, fuck that, can we have a steak now L.O.L.

I would always enjoy when Troy visited because he would always leave plenty on his plate and often Dad would shout from the kitchen, "hope you haven't just given Stella all that food you left" Ha-ha. Of course he had "Silly Bollox" and I had devoured it and wiped my arse with the Weight Watchers Diplomas; high five to Troy; my favourite Family member.

CHAPTER FIFTEEN

Dad had recently had visitors in the shape of Ken Loach the Film Director and his friend Paul Laverty; to discuss the ins and outs of the infamous bedroom tax. Someone had spoken to Ken whilst he visited the most controversial and complex person that he would need to meet was my Dad, Dave Ginnelly. I don't think any of us are in disagreement there do you L.O.L.? Thankfully, it was one of Dads better days and he talked sensible and kept his clothes on throughout. Ken liked Dad that much; he placed his name in the credits at the end of his latest award winning film, I Daniel Blake. I don't think it is any coincidence that because Dad has friends in high places that he is left alone more and more with regard to his situation.

Very strange and especially because I had notified them that Ken was more than a little interested in the outcome of any of their "supposed expert medical examinations" and everything seems fine for now with no sanctions whatsoever. It seems natural that I and Dad are destined for fame, he has his name in credits in movies and we both write books. He gets invited to speak to the women at the Institute and even speaks about my books, because dogs are not allowed in the Chess Centre up Camp Hill. I'm sure it would be a good idea to smuggle me inside a box full of books and I can just jump out and tap dance and fox trot for all the ladies. They would soon realise that I am much better company than "Silly Bollox" and as I stated earlier I am sure he upset a few of them on a previous visit. It's simply a case of everyone realising he is speaking of a Dave Ginnelly in a previous decade and not the one he lives in now.

Don't get me wrong, he still needs you all to pray for him and he misses eating all of your baked cakes and I wouldn't mind sampling some of them now that I'm off my diet. If the Police hadn't smashed our door in and taken our cannabis tent, we could have all got a good business venture going between us and made some proper "Space Cakes". We could have run the whole town, Dad could have provided the produce and all you girls in your aprons and oven gloves could have done the baking. We could have won no end of Awards and Diplomas as best newcomers in the caking making department. That would have been until we all got our doors knocked and Dad denied knowing any of you, apart from coming and talking about his books. Don't any of you worry though because we would visit you on remand, I can see the headlines in all of the newspapers now? WOMENS INSTITUTE SPACED OUT! God Bless you ladies and we hope you are all doing well.

172

Dad still keeps in touch with Ken Loach and even on the night he made history winning an Award for the second time in the South of France Cannes Film Festival, for I Daniel Blake. Dad had dropped him a text congratulating him and even though he would have been a busy man that night he replied within fifteen minutes. That's because people like him and Paul are true and genuine and don't ever play the fame game in life they are the sort of people that I truly admire and respect. They are welcome to come up to the Women's Institute and have tea and cake anytime they wish. Dad said I'm not allowed any cake in case I get the "munchies" the bastard him; how cruel is he?

Dad was quite famous in his own right now due to the success of his first book WELLIES AND WARDERS, which had gone straight to number one on Amazon forty-eight hours after its release. It had sold in fourteen countries and gained critical acclaim and made him a very proud man. The amount of Royalties he received each month from Amazon meant we could live the high life a little. For some strange reason he thought salmon was an indication of wealth because I seemed to have salmon every time I looked in my bowl. Jesus, did he think I was a cat now? Perhaps if he gave it more thought he could realise that's where my weight problems began.

I did get a little jealous of his books and so that's why I wrote my own because he is more of a serious natured writer, whereas I like to let loose and tap dance through life. I'm not here for as long as the rest of you BUT while I'm here, for that short period, I will leave you all with a lasting impression of STELLA GINNELLY Nuneaton's Wonder Dog. Everyone will now be able to read about my adventures and my memory will last for many years yet. Nobody will ever forget me and "Silly Bollox" as we are certainly among the town's characters and we are certainly a dying breed.

Dad has carried quite a few coffins lately and is always asked because it's an honour to carry someone, especially if they have touched peoples' lives. Darren Carter was one of these special people, who gave homeless people his last few pounds on a regular basis and left himself without a penny. Dad had always said KENNY KITBAG was one of the nicest people he had ever met and was such a loveable character. That he won't never let his memory fade and it deeply touched him that his Mum had asked him to be one of the Pall Bearers because he felt proud to do so. I bet all of you up Camp Hill have missed Kenny running round the Estate mowing your gardens for you for the price of a bottle of wine and gave you lots of laughs while he mowed away. I loved that lad and yes maybe he had his own issues and demons but all he ever showed any of you was a whole heap of kindness. Kenny's issues were alcohol and Dads are drugs but it doesn't make either of them bad people. I would love to see Kenny in the town always running to hug Dad with his bottle of whatever in his hand always full of love. The town will always miss and remember you Kenny, sparkle and shine fella. My Dad will always keep your memory alive.

I love living in Nuneaton and especially with Dad because there isn't anybody who he does not know. He is so warmly greeted by everyone and that now rubs off on me because everyone knows who I am as well. A perfect pairing are me and "Silly Bollox". Not that we had discussed it but I can imagine Dad sniffing my ashes, I can remember him laughing when he heard Keith Richards from the Rolling Stones had sniffed a family members ashes and I knew that idea would have stuck in his head. The daft twat might get a shock and the way his is living right now it might be me that sniffs his ashes and buries him out in the woods. Especially if he puts me on another of his fucking diets because I might give him one of his hammers around his head. I could quite easily manage by myself and "Silly Bollox" needs to realise that. I know how to open the door and come and go, plus all of the local shops know me and I could soon source some money from somewhere if I went back to being a bit shady. So you see he would be no great loss. Oh, so ok, I wouldn't know how to use the hoover or the iron but I'm a little dog so what the fuck would I want to switch an iron on for.

I had more pressing matters because my daughter Millie who lived with Adam Green, was being a bit of a bitch and staying out sleeping around and had already made me a Grandma once. Adam didn't know what to do with her, so I put that on my to-do list. It had stressed me out that much that I took a few of Dads Sertraline. They were his very serious top end anti depressants but I wouldn't take too many OR who would babysit him for the rest of the day.

There did not seem to be too much of anything positive happening. Then the postman arrived and he brought an invite to the wedding reception of Charlie Bronson Salvador to Paula Salvador at a hotel opposite Wakefield prison and the gathering would only be for a select few and I saw there was a plus one on there so was presuming I would need a new outfit. Later that evening I heard Dad speaking to his friend Mark White.... Mr Not Quite Right, the very same lunatic who had knocked the Lucky Lucky Men out in Tenerife. To be honest a very unpredictable and volatile character that seemed destined to be taking my place. I do not think so Mr White! No way was I being left behind because I had planned on catching the flowers when Paula throws them.

When the time arrived in November 2017, the three of us travelled up by train. The plan was I was staying with Mick Fox while that pair of fucking idiots were getting a taxi to Wakefield from Dewsbury. Nobody had even noticed that I had slipped into the taxi and concealed myself; while those pair talked complete garbage, with all of the incoherent ramblings; it was obvious they had taken cocaine. I ran into the York House Hotel, while they paid the cab fare and straight past the Security unnoticed. I was that small and by the time my company entered the room I was sat up on a chair with a glass of Babycham and just gave the pair of them the middle finger.

Lots of other people were there as couples, as in man and wife but this pair just looked like a pair of gaylords. On reflection I had even seen Whity earlier plucking the longer hairs on Dads eyebrows and how gay is that L.O.L. The guests were few because it was a very private guest list and only one hundred and fifty had been invited and Dad knew few of them. Dave Courtney was there along with one of the Richardson's and Alex Reid the cross dressing cage fighter that married Katie Price. Alex seemed a nice bloke to be fair and we only had Katie's version of events in their marriage and what took place. Dad looked around to see if he knew anyone else and I kept waving to let him know that he knew me L.O.L. There were certainly a few of London's underworld in attendance but all in all it was a friendly atmosphere and no trouble took place because the waiting Media outside would have loved that.

Out of all the characters that were there and known faces; Dad was most impressed with meeting Mike O'Hagan who years and years before had been Charlie's lock down Officer, he was the very first Prison Officer to show Charlie any kindness. Sometimes in an Institution that's the one thing that breaks down barriers. Just through the few fleeting conversations Dad had with him it was plain to see he was kind natured.

I kept my eyes on my Dad at all times, as he would have been chasing the women down. I had watched him eyeing all of the talent up at the other side of the room, Beverley Zacher, Star Harris and Julie Preston. He had heard Julie had even been a Prison Officer, in one of Hulls Prisons, I bet my Dad wouldn't have said no to her locking his cell door. It was a happy occasion with lot of fun and laughter and eyebrow plucking from Whity but alas the wedding was to be an ill fated one; as I will tell you in one of the later chapters. God Bless you on this day Paula looking beautiful and glowing with happiness.

CHAPTER SIXTEEN

It was an eventful journey back to Nuneaton, as I watched Dad and Whity doing a Westlife and Flying Without Wings. The emptied the buffet trolley of vodka and then started on the gin and this was only going to end up one way. Yes that's right; we ended up two stops past our Tamworth train station and out in the sticks somewhere. The Ticket Guard was astounded when Whity asked him had we reached Tamworth yet, and stood with his mouth open as they got off at the next station and doubled back, albeit having added one and a half hours to their journey. As they got off, he shook his head in disbelief, but if he even knew a fraction of what this pair got up to on their travels, he would then see today's excursion as just a slight misdemeanour. This pair was the Butch Cassidy and Sundance Kid of the railways, motorways and even plane flights. If there was drama to be had this pair of fucking idiots would find it.

I never got the chance to see Paula, or grab the flowers and say goodbye but after giving it a little thought I wasn't sure I wanted a partner again to be honest. I had only ever had the one lover another Jack Russell called Bud and I can assure you that Bud never made the earth move. We had been introduced on a few occasions and the odd brushing of heads would always be accompanied with the obligatory sniff at the rear end. Jesus! This dog would do more sniffing than my Dad on a weekend. He had obviously never done it before and I was younger than him and had not had any experience myself. Although, I was experienced enough to know that Bud, bless his heart, was having difficulty finding the hole. If he couldn't find the hole then he was going to struggle to find the elusive G spot wasn't he? I would safely say the ONLY spot Bud hit was a flat spot.

We had pups but nothing about the actual bonding would have been described as memorable and it had put me off, ever finding another partner. I still see Bud occasionally, when I visit where he lives, he is a little older and wiser now. I'd guess and aware of what to do but every time he dives off the sofa with his little pecker popping out. I soon dampen his spirits, when I give the exposed part a rake with my longest and sharpest nail; it soon pops back in like a tortoise in its shell. "Put it away Bud" now there's a good boy.

So he didn't feel too upset and rejected I told him maybe another time, because today I just felt a little weak because I had recently been on a diet. He seemed happy enough with that explanation and after I gave him a kiss on his forehead, he jumped back on the settee and went to sleep.

I was a career girl now I was going to apply to be a Drug Counsellor and if they wanted to know if I had any experience. I would just need to write on the Application Form, I HAVE LIVED WITH DAVE GINNELLY FOR TEN YEARS. I was sure nobody would have more experience than that and especially taking into account, that I would need to put up with many of his friends when they stayed overnight.

Dad has got a big marble fireplace with a very wide shelf and I would bounce up there from the trampoline. People I tell you no lies, the things I have witnessed from that shelf, would make your toes curl up or your ribs crack with laughing. I would just lean on my elbow, look from one face to another, and it would be very difficult to pick the idiot of the night because they were all complete arseholes. I stood as much chance as anyone else of getting the job. To promote my case further, I would show them a photo of myself as a Nun, outside St Paulinus Church and just hope they didn't check with Father Hinchcliffe.

I couldn't believe I had been thrown out of the Church, after they had discovered details about my love, daughter, because it wasn't as if she had been dumped. She lived with my good friend Adam Green, but in all honesty she had begun to put it out a bit herself and had made me a Grandma. It just seemed Jack Russell's were shagging all over the oche. It wouldn't have looked good, my daughter getting pregnant at an early age. Perhaps, it was for the best because I'm not sure I could have handled the vow of silence if I'm truthful. With my vast experience, my time would be better served helping youngsters with drug issues, on the plus side I could bring home to Dad all of the drugs I had confiscated from any of my clients.

We needed at least one wage coming in because I was a typical girl who enjoyed my grooming at Shampooches Boutique up Camp Hill, where Sal Stroud and Brad Webb always gave me the best treatment in Nuneaton. I found them on Facebook and have never used anybody else since. I would want to look my smartest soon, because I had read a few of my Dads messages on his phone. It appeared we were about to march on Downing Street or the Justice Department to hand in a 20,000 signature petition, demanding the release of Charlie. I raced to my room to start making my own placards which I would surprise Dad with on the day, once I had hidden them in my Scooby Doo suitcase. Whity was meant to be going with him again, but Dad had second thoughts about taking him down to the Capital; just because his presence increased the odds of being arrested. There was a lot of on-line activity over the coming weeks and I had noted everything I could remember; while I sat on the top of his shoulder resting on the settee. I could always be found strolling along, on the top of the three piece suite. I had the attributes of a cat as I would leap from chair to chair.

It was an event to look forward to when Dad went to the pub, he would try and encourage other people to go and he came home with a girl called Angela, if I recall correctly, "Silly Bollox" had been taken in again by a member of the female sex. Every time Dad spoke of Charlie or indicated for her to read his funny postcards her indifference was plain to see. Well to everyone but Dad that was! I sat and watched her closely and saw what a devious little person she was. Dad went to the toilet and very hurriedly she took a small clip bay out of her handbag, she delicately place one of her garishly painted finger nails in and sniffed the contents very carefully; it was obvious she had done this many times before. She may have thought she looked very elegant the way she had done it but she was the least ladylike female, I'd seen for a long time. She obviously had no intention of sharing, for that reason alone, she was about to lose the remainder of her powder; as soon as she took her eyes off her handbag. I watched her rambling constantly which at least confirmed that it was cocaine rather than ketamine, which many of the local young girls had been consuming for a while lately.

I just sidled along the arm of the chair and pretended to lose my balance and fall; any doubts I had that I was doing the wrong thing soon disappeared with the sound of laughter coming from Angela's mouth, at my supposed misfortune in falling. Jesus Christ! She sounded like a donkey, for fucks sake somebody give her a carrot. I had done what I had set out to do and had the bag and its contents firmly in my paw and secreted it under the stairs where I occasionally slept, If I wanted to chill out alone or Dad had brought an "Angela" home with him.

The silly girl kept laughing at me over and over and I would just glare at her. It soon became my own turn to smirk as once again Dad went to the toilet again, she quickly reached for her bag, becoming very anxious the longer she could not find it and I sniggered to myself while I sat in the chair opposite her.

When Dad came back it all became a little embarrassing for my little eyes to witness the heavy petting that was going off and the clothes flying through the air as they undressed and ravished each other. I should have recorded it to show Bud my previous and only lover, what to do and the exact procedure. Instead I retired to my room under the stairs and pushed the door shut a little to dull the noise because now Angela was braying like a donkey.

I must have fell asleep because when I awoke it was the early hours of the morning, as I drifted into the living room, it was clear that the "lady" was still here as her clothes were strewn everywhere. I did not hide the fact that I disliked this one and I set about ripping her panties with my teeth. She might not have shown up with crotch less panties but she was definitely leaving wearing a pair. My treat Angela, enjoy, because I would certainly get Dad to enjoy your bag.

The day came for the march in London and off we went dad pulling his designer case and me with my Scooby Doo pull along, we must have looked a funny sight down at Euston Train Station. Dad looked around outside, I knew he had many sad memories of being homeless and sleeping outside this very Station; when he was a young boy. He would come looking for the homeless later, before we departed but for now there were more pressing matters.

I had given him the clip bag over the breakfast table before we had set off and it soon became apparent what a mistake that had been, as he had soon partaken and his confused face said it all. As we went round and round in circles on the tube and got lost; I felt like Scott of the Antarctic going round and round. This was going to be one of them occasions when I would need the dog lead on him rather than the other way round. Eventually, we landed at Westminster and left the tube station, everything is very double quick time down there and everyone in a rush. Nobody has time to stop and give directions, so Dad took the easy option and flagged a taxi down. We just got settled in the cab and out of the rain when the driver said "where to Governor" and when Dad replied "Saint Stephens Tavern" the driver looked at Dad like he was a lunatic; then pointed straight across the road and there in all its glory was the pub he had been looking for. A classic Dad routine in my eyes I had seen his lunacy often enough and had had many laughs but for the past forty minutes he had stood in the rain OUTSIDE Saint Stephens Tavern, off his nut, asking people for directions to the very building L.O.L. I bet the taxi driver wanted to boot him up his arse, being that he had just been crossing the bridge, had been flagged down and needed to turn around. He drove away with his middle finger up to Dad, but because Dad did not have his glasses on he simply thought he was waving and waved back and said "he was a nice chap Stella"!

I was glad I had come down with him because there were likely to be a few more situations yet. He still had more cocaine and once he had a little alcohol on top of that, he would be stripping off and dancing in this rain, which showed no sign of stopping and seemed to be here for the day. We went into the pub and he ordered his customary pint for himself, but I told him I weren't bothered for a babycham as it would probably cost a fortune down here.

I also had it in my head to remain sober, as I would need to keep an eye on the drink intake of "Silly Bollox"; who becomes a nightmare after six pints. There was a lot of waving from some pretty girls in the corner and i waved back because he hadn't even seen them wave. I was ever so pleased to realise these were the friends we were meeting, although, I did not like the look of a few of them which in time turned out to be a correct decision in later days when they sold Charlie/Paula out to the media for 30 pieces of silver

CHAPTER SEVENTEEN

Some of the people we met that day have become long standing friends. Not all of those were in attendance for the march; I met many of them at the wedding, which was on a selective invite only.

The ones on the march were genuine supporters of Charlie. Rod and Linda Harrison who are tireless in all their efforts they put in for Charlie. Andrew Parkin and his good lady who had come from Sunderland and was an artist himself and had made placards for everyone, I would surprise them all once I got my own out.

Timothy Douglas Crowley and his lovely wife Diane Scriven Sunshine JoJo a mad head from Brighton, Beverleigh Zacher who is a top girl. Julian Foster and his wife Paula Frankland, young Scouse lad John James, Matt Barber a good lad from Lincoln. All of these were beautiful people along with others who could not make it on the day, but I would get a chance to meet, at a later time Daz Holcroft, Ivor Batty, Chris Staffy Stafford and any others that we may have overlooked. Every one of you has been a pleasure to meet along the way.

On this day there were also two people in attendance that were like chalk and cheese in comparison to each other. It was obviously a delicate situation but I am entitled to my opinion and so is Dad. In the corner of the pub with a big glowing smile that just welcomed you instantly was Paula Salvador, Charlie's wife, who had loved all of the stories to do with me and said I was the funniest dog ever and she had even shared photos of me with her parents. Nobody doubts that Paula had a few issues God Bless her but her heart was in the right place. She was devoted to getting Charlie realised and that it will always make me see Paula in a different light to what others did. I will discuss Paula in a later chapter.

Also on that day we had the repulsive task of meeting a certain George Bamby Salvador because he was claiming to be Charlie's son. I could see Dad looking him up and down in his camouflage clothes and even the image he presented was shabby; anyone of you would be hard pushed to find an individual more low life that this person. I am prepared to state here and now that YOU ARE NOT Charlie's son and if you wish to sue for libel then be my guest. For you to travel to Wales, place your arm around Charlie's Mum and to keep up the pretence sickens me. How dare you do that to an old lady and cause the confusion that you have. Who would even want to go to the lengths? My Dad cannot believe he stood in the company of a man such as yourself and you still keep up the pretence now on-line! My Dads got mental health issues but no way to the extent that you have in your imaginary world. You are a shyster, an imposter and it angers me that you dared place an arm on Charlie's Mum.

Once we had left the pub and set off on the march I got my placard out of my case and I thought Dad would be happy. As I had always heard him call Maggie Thatcher for what she did to the Miners during the Strike and I had a big cartoon painting of her with the words THATCHER OFF WITH HER HEAD. I held it up aloft and thought people would cheer but Dad whispered in my ear that she had died many years before. This news angered me and I wanted to smash the placard over this George's head, but I tripped him up instead, while he was on the floor I bit into his ankle and gathered some of the hairs on his leg in between my teeth. After we had the hairs sent for a DNA test, the nearest match we could find was a Rat or a Snake; definitely vermin.

By the way this man still uses the family name to conduct business on-line, selling prints of Charlie's art; should any of my friends still be in any form of contact with this man than wash your hands of him. He is very much a fraudster who invents names. His name is not Salvador and he is NO relation whatsoever to Charlie. Spread the word far and wide. Who killed Bamby? It sounds like a Disney film; he is definitely a Disney character. I wish he had one of the big chains around his neck that Rappers have and I wished if you pulled it he flushed away like a turd; but I am afraid you are likely to be stuck with that leach for many years yet.

It was an enjoyable day apart from his presence and thankfully he never came to the pub afterwards. I had seen Dad looking at him deep and meaningful and Bamby would be wise to stay out of harms reach where my Dads concerned. It's lucky he has all of them cameras and binoculars around his neck, as he will need them to make sure Dad isn't approaching. Anyway, enough about a shallow twat like that it is not worth the ink in this pen.

Hey, I am aware this is meant to be a funny book but life is not that simple I'm afraid. You all know what Dads like when he thinks something's unjust and it don't come more unjust than forty-four years in a cell and sometimes the only people you see are snakes and vipers. Anyway, Dads told me if I don't cover Charlie's story he will put me back on the dreaded Tuna/Salmon carry on, or worse still the Atkins Diet and I never wanted to see a tomato again as long as I lived. So there you are Charlie B. Your wish is my command.

Someone just shouted the Jagers up, so I jumped from table to table high fiving everyone until I could drink no more and suggested we go and do a little sightseeing.

Many of the others had overnight accommodation in London but we would need to catch one of the last trains back to Nuneaton, albeit travelling first class, because Dads friend PIP Crowder, had prepaid for us to have comfortable travel arrangements. Life could be like that around Dad because he had a network of people who took an interest in his welfare. It must be nice for him to feel appreciated b others the way that he is because they support him in many ways.

After saying our goodbyes until the next time. We once again made for the unenviable tube journey OR journeys, which is more often the case and yet again we went round and round in circles, the only difference this time was I was pissed on the Jagers I had drank. I would need to snap out of it quickly though because "Silly Bollox" was not only pissed but wired with it, which was a lethal combination as I watched him singing Fleetwood Mac songs and spinning in circles. He wasn't even looking for our tube station, so I needed to assume command and regain some order. I would welcome a cold shower right now so I settled for a cold swim and in a flash Trafalgar Square hit my head like a brainstorm. I knew my placards would come in handy because I had brought two with Dad and I, he had roared when I got the other one out of my case as it had a picture of Winston Churchill and a demand for him to be put back in office. "For fucks sake Stella" Dad howled and poked fun at me, which was out of order to be honest, because I'm only a dog and can't be expected to know everything.

I took one of the laces out of his trainers, while he was rolling about laughing and secured it to the side of what I class as the Crème de la Crème of fountains (I've been in plenty); the one I call Terrific Trafalgar. Dad sat down to rest his drunken head and I gently went to the very tip of the placard and after a couple of gentle springs up and down; I leaped upwards like a gazelle and plummeted into the water. Instantly I felt refreshed as I hit the cold water and I swam around gleefully as I was at my happiest when I was in water. There are thousands of photographs of me in water in the North, South, East and West of the country. In another life I could quite easily have been a dolphin the amount of time I spent swimming.

I didn't dare risk any longer than half an hour in case Dad got bored and forgot I was with him and simply walked off. Trust me, it wouldn't have been the first time he had done so. He may have been the worse for wear but I was suitably refreshed now and completely back in the game.

We headed towards Euston and along the way stopping at different shops to purchase alcohol, cigarettes, tobacco, toiletries and a few bottles of fresh water. We were about to enter the real world of London rather than the tourist one that many of you see. Dad was amazed to find, that in the exact place where he had slept in a dirty old mailbag when he was a teenager fourteen years of age, there was a young couple with a tent put up and many others had done the same close by surrounding areas. This was the reality of modern day Britain, not a lot had changed since 1969 to be truthful and it anything the situation had worsened. The young boy said he was from Burnley and the girl didn't want to say and I respected her wishes. I could remember Dad saying that he became very secretive when he was on the Streets and private details were not to be shared. We went into the Station and got them both a Cornish pasty at a cost of £5.20 each, money was no object to Dad but Jesus it had become costly to be homeless in London. We gave them all the extras we had bought earlier and they both ate the pies while Dad talked of historical days spent in this spot.

They ate greedily as was to be expected and they could not stop shaking his hand in thanks for the amount of extras he had lavished on them.

In life we will all meet people who constantly have their hands out and give nothing in return. We had already seen this couple go from tent to tent sharing the cigarettes and cans; it brought back memories of the kindness of random strangers had shown him. We were running to a tight schedule now and would need to leave shortly; as Dad shook the man's hand he gave him the remaining contents of clip bag. Some of you may be shocked by that but when you are on the Street you usually have nothing for company other than drugs or alcohol. It's not for any of you to question or judge that because we all of us have situations that put us in that place. We all have demons and not everybody lives a trouble free comfortable life and it's best to remember that.

Dads policy in life is he refuses to look up to anybody at all and for sure he never looks down on anybody either. We were about to come across one of the perfect examples, as we boarded the train home and took our seat in the first class compartment. When some condescending twat with a Scouse accent said "hey mate, this is first class", Dad just smiled at him and went back to drinking his can of cider.

He had had a lovely day doing lots of good and positive things and was feeling pleased; when the speaker echoed with the voice of the Guard saying "anyone who shouldn't be in first class, please leave now". It was blatantly obvious that it was directed at us and Dads appearance and in particular his heavily tattooed hands. When the female Guard entered the carriage she made no pretence of looking at anyone's tickets and made a beeline for Dad. "Tickets please" she said in a demanding voice and Dad informed her upon producing his ticket that he could report her for discriminating against him. Instead he stood up called everyone in the carriage a bunch of shallow bastards and informed them of the good news that we were only travelling as far as Nuneaton and they would soon be rid of us. We then went and stood in the corridor for the next forty-five minutes until we reached Nuneaton

CHAPTER EIGHTEEN

Judgemental people hey! None of us need them sort although from a judging point someone had been filling Dads head with thoughts of stardom and told him to really consider it because Simon Cowell loved dog acts. When Dad had mentioned it to a friend they had stupidly asked "why what can Stella do"? He got given a very firm lecture and a breakdown of how I could sing, tap dance, do gymnastics and under water tricks. A genuine all rounder of the canine world but I said to him I thought it was a secret me being able to talk, so the singing was definitely out.

He became very reflective; I took a seat and watched while his eyes and brain began to assess his idea. Eventually his "eureka" moment came and he had to work out how we could BOTH become famous and suggested a ventriloquist act like Lord Snooty and Charles. We bounced the idea about a little until the reality of it all kicked in. Whoa! Just a fucking minute, will this involve you putting your hand up my arse OR anywhere near my arse, come to that. We will need to make it look authentic he said, as casually as you like, as if it was the most normal thing ever. I shook my head over and over and made it clear that it was not happening on my shift. That was not now and not never with a capital N. For a start who would find it a bit difficult talking, let alone singing with a fist stuck all the way up your arse and half way up your back. "Gottle of Geer, Gottle of Geer", no way! I'm ever so sorry "Silly Bollox" but it's a nonstarter and we won't be staying at the judges' house which is a big plus to be honest because you might get Louis Walsh putting a fist up

YOUR arse during the night and it would be nothing to do with ventriloquism.

We would need to find another source of income but even that would have to wait because I was not feeling well at all; I had broken out in a rash. Someone had warned Dad not to let me in any of the water that was around the Cockneys because they were a funny lot who ate eels for fucks sake! "Strange People" Dads mate had said; all a little cor blimey and Mary Poppins and a little bit too much for me.

Dad wasted no time in getting over to the P.D.S.A. I truly loved all of the people who worked here and they did a load of allergy tests and we would need to wait a few days. True to their word they rang DAD in the next forty-eight hours. They could not stop laughing as they informed him that I was allergic to rabbits and the laugh at the other end became hysterical as the lady put the phone down as she collapsed in a fit of giggling. News soon filtered out to other people and within the hour I was grabbing all the headlines JACK RUSSELL ALLERGIC TO RABBITS. Why me for fucks sake, I had become an internet sensation with everyone having a laugh at my expense. Jesus Christ, it was like Charlie Bronson being allergic to a cell! The door knocking constantly and that was no good and especially for my Dads paranoia so we packed a few things and rolled up the tent, grabbed the bus pass and off us went.

No internet where we were going, complete peace and rest in the middle of a field somewhere. Although having said that this daft twat could find trouble in the middle of anywhere. The Vet had also noted I seemed a little down and had prescribed anti depressants for me, it turned out both of us were taking Sertraline. So God knows what path this would lead us down. Dad also had a wheelbarrow full of other mind altering substances to take each day, so I would still need to be able to function myself and care for his needs. I would need to keep that very private, or social media would be like a bush fire, with stories of a rabbit fearing terrier on medication and I'd gone through enough ridicule the last few days.

We didn't have to travel too far because there are plenty of picturesque areas in and around Warwickshire. We pitched a tent and made it very homely for our overnight stay, then got a small fire going with a little stone circle around it, to stop the fire spreading. We had our most peaceful night for a long while and we revelled in each other's company as it had been a while since it was just us two.

Dad was always like everyone's Social Worker/Parole Officer/Citizens Advice or even Samaritans. The poor bloke never got a minute but there was nowhere here to charge a phone and it's what we both needed; a few days of complete seclusion. I bet Dad missed the privacy of solitary confinement in the jail, as he always laughed to people who said that prison was hard back in the "old days". As he couldn't wait to play up and get sent down the block, to get him a single cell instead of sharing with two others. I'd got him with me now though and no way would he be going back in there ever again.

He was stood in the middle of the little brook the following morning and I originally thought he was having a wash until he informed me that he was waiting to tickle a trout or a salmon L.O.L. You couldn't make it up with this bloke and I giggled all the way back to the camp and thought it would be nigh on impossible to meet a bigger nutcase than him.

Than as if I had set myself a challenge, a very hearty "Good Morning", boomed out from in front of me, as he waved to Dad. Here stood a very eccentric looking Farmer, with what I can only describe as a blunderbuss, resting on his shoulder and for sure that would spread buckshot far and wide. As he was talking to Dad, he must have spotted something move out of the corner of his eye, in an instant he had dropped to one knee and pulled the trigger. It was the funniest thing I had ever seen, as the recoil of the gun knocked him off his feet. "Did I hit it" he enquired, hit what I thought; I hadn't seen a thing to be truthful? Then demanded that I FETCH ha-ha, I looked behind me where nobody stood and I found it comical that he definitely was saying it to me. This now confirmed to me that he was a very silly man, albeit with a good nature, as he invited us up to the farmhouse, to have a little breakfast with him and his wife.

Whilst we walked to the farm, he dropped to his knee again and fired away rapidly with a catapult and Jesus Christ. It seemed he only needed a bow and arrow now and a spear and his armoury would be complete. Although, it seemed a funny thought, I would not bet against him having the additional weaponry back at his home. He was still a child at heart and his wife kissed him tenderly on his forehead as he informed her that he hadn't caught anything. "Never mind Dear, sit down and have your breakfast"!

We all exchanged pleasantries, then Mrs Hargreaves put the biggest tray I had ever seen in front of me and I imagined that to be share among the four of us, until she patted my head and said "tuck in dear". I didn't need telling twice and the diet was soon forgotten about. I could see Dad looking angry at the amount I was eating and he knew it couldn't be helped because if he said anything it would be regarded as rude. So it was I cleared the massive plate, obviously only out of politeness and I would need to roll to the big open fire, as I was too full to walk.

Halfway through the meal, Mr Hargreaves must have sighted something again out of the kitchen window; he jumped up and fired his catapult out of the window. None of us knew if he had hit his target or not, BUT we were sure Mrs Hargreaves had definitely hit her target, as she very swiftly clipped her husband around the ear and told him to get sat back at the table. He sat very forlorn like a chastised child as he dipped his toast in his egg yolk and it transpired that they had been married forty years and I wondered how many times in that period of time she would have struck that very same ear L.O.L.

She would more than likely let him play out with his "toys" during the morning and his afternoons would be spent driving the combine harvester from one field to another. It seemed a very idyllic lifestyle, although, they both expressed their concerns at the impending Brexit and where it would leave them as regards continuing to be able to make a living. We thanked them wholeheartedly for the breakfast, as we had been starving and we would have waited all day for "Silly Bollox" to tickle a trout, as he hadn't a clue what to actually do. It was something he had read about and the daft twat thinks that's enough to make it a reality.

We cleaned up any mess we had left at the bottom of the field and looked across to the other field to wave to Mr Hargreaves. Just in time to see him apply the brake to the harvester and dive out of the cab whilst firing yet another shot from his catapult as he rolled like James Bond in the soil. It was comical to watch and he was older than Dad and I thought that his eyesight would be as bad as Dads, if not worse. I doubted the other Farmers minded because he probably harvested the wrong fields on many occasions and did their work for them by mistake.

Dad had to dive quickly as we made our way across the field we were in as a few pieces of lead shot whistled past. He had obviously seen us moving out of the corner of his eye and so we would be fair game and a possible kill. It was as if he was constantly on safari, but if Mrs Hargreaves brought him sandwiches later, he would find himself getting another clip, if she knew he was still playing with his toys.

We hit the main road and saw the signs for Kenilworth and Fillongley, we headed in that direction, until we got our bearings to get us homeward bound. We weren't hitching a lift and didn't even have a thumb out when a car pulled up by us and the Driver laughed loudly, as he stated "fuck me, yes, I thought it was you Poppa G". As many of the younger ones called Dad as he fathered them all in his own little way.

It was Frosty who I really liked as he always made a fuss of me. Jason Frost was one of Dads good mates and a bit of a player and always back and forth to Thailand every two minutes. He told Dad he had started his own car valeting business and he had called it "A Touch of Frost" which we all laughed at because it was a quality title. Jason got us in the car with him, none of us were in a rush to get back to Nuneaton and we had a tour around a couple of countryside pubs and had something to eat. Much of the conversation was suggesting Dad got himself a Bride from Thailand, I would glare and Frosty would say "look at jealous eyes on her" and then stated she is like your wife Poppa G instead of your Daughter. I laughed at it all anyway, because knowing how bad Dads were, it was a nailed on certainty that any dating he did out there, would turn out to be a chick with a dick. He wouldn't have a clue what to do out there.

Frosty was a seasoned veteran in the department and would be buffing more that cars while he was out that neck of the woods. It was good to see him, but it had been a long day and we were all of us ready for our beds by the time we were dropped off at home.

CHAPTER NINETEEN

It was a strange carry on, not like I was complaining. I'd had a rough start in life and was passed around like an orphan Annie BUT I'd finally come through with flying colours and everyone absolutely loved me. Well you could say every man and his dog did L.O.L. Everywhere I walked in the town or on the Estate, I would get greeted warmly and it was as if I had been given the freedom of the city. I would hop on and off all of the buses even if I was by myself and never needed to pay. If I passed any of the local Butchers they would run out to ask "how's your Dad", and throw me a bone or a juicy titbit? This was it now, I'd got just the life that I wished for and I was sure that I have earned all of this respect along the way.

I had contributed to charitable causes and also slept rough over night to raise much needed funds for the homeless teenagers at Doorway. I had done it with Dad and we had made quite a bit of money between us. We were meant to be doing it again sometime soon but I was dreading it causing problems with Dad, as he is older that God's dog right now and it wouldn't make sense him making himself ill but it won't stop me from doing it. Many others are meant to be sleeping out for the night at Nuneaton's Football Club Ground. The club was now managed by Dads brother Jimmy Ginnelly; we would often have a Jager and a high five because we were proud of what he has achieved.

All of us in our own right had become a little famous because Dad had a sister Susan who was an accomplished musician and Dad and I both wrote books and Jimmy's managerial position at Nuneaton was the pinnacle of his career and his name was legendary in non league football.

I would be recognised everywhere I went and people would wave or point from passing buses and half the time they would be staring because of my antics rather than who I was. As I would be walking on my front legs doing a handstand while my back legs would be in the air spinning a Lucozade bottle around. I never did things normally, I was the sort of dog that clamoured for a little entertainment and could always be seen performing one trick or another. If I had talent it was pointless hiding it and I used to love watching people's jaws drop with surprise. At least they knew all of us now for all the right reasons.

"Silly Bollox" had not even been in a courtroom for twenty-five years now, let alone been in a prison. Although, if I am to be frank God has smiled on him plenty and he had led a charmed life at time. On the whole he is respected and that rubs off on me. God was certainly looking down on me with this lunatic; we are certainly a match made in heaven. We were a familiar sight everywhere we went around the Estate and would practically live on the canal tow path we spent that much time there.

We would come off occasionally and go onto one of the many Estates in the area; more often than not we would go to see his good mate Rafael Viola. That in itself was a challenge for me because he was a Spanish Glaswegian and his accent made it difficult to understand what he was saying. Even his own Smart Phone could not grasp what tongue he was talking in. Rafael was the same as Dad and had spent many years, albeit for a miscarriage of justice, he received twelve years imprisonment for a charge of joint enterprise; which in effect says that if you are at the scene you are guilty by means of association. Raff was in a completely different room to his brothers, when somebody got stabbed, to death with a bayonet and even though Rafael was in that other room and not even aware of an argument all the accused were given twelve years imprisonment. He went on hunger strikes and other protests but nothing could be done because of the law surrounding such cases. It's a case that needs to be looked at with regard to exonerating his name as a murderer. Raff's no murderer; he is a very nice man; that's when I can understand a word he is saying.

He is not a well man right now and sleeps in a hospital bed in his living room. I can always be found under that bed hiding things and it's always got to be right in the corner and I push it up really tight using my nose. However, on this day I had gone under and set about retrieving one of the treats I had hidden under the darkened bed. Raff is a regular cannabis smoker and he must have spilled his jar and when I was rummaging about in the dark my mouth made contact with what seemed like a crispy delicacy and I wasted no time eating it. Whatever it was it had a strange earthy taste to it and I struggled to walk and I wouldn't be juggling many Lucozade bottles right now. I had eaten a good sized bud of the finest skunk weed that we around at the time and once the initial shock had worn away and I was completely numb; I had to agree that it was much better than chewing on a Bonio or a doggy dental stick. Having said that I wasn't in a rush to chew another one but I was enjoying the experience L.O.L.

Dad would see Raff's needs because his legs had almost completely given up on him and Dad would need to be his legs for him. I used to joke that in return Raff would be Dads eyes and ears because nothing worked right on him. His brain would certainly need assistance, you could soak that in Steradent overnight and it would still not function. Dad would never let Raff down for nothing, it was much better in life, to have that one good friend you can rely on; rather than sit amongst the fakes who call you in your absence. Keep your circle tight and keep it real is the only way to be.

For now I was pleasantly drifting around the living room, with a warm glow about myself, in future I would bring items out in the light before I consumed them again. When we walked home down the canal, for a change the last thing I wanted to do was dive in and swim the short hop back to the flats. I was still aware enough to do my duties because we worked as a team and I went up the stairwell first and barked constantly to make Dad aware that someone was knocking at our flat.

This was a well worked out routine, as Dad arrived at the top of the stairs we both just ambled past the very officious looking person at the door and past our own door with Dad declaring to the man and his clip board that the resident of the flat was very rarely there and he had heard he worked away in Europe quite a lot. While he was informing him of this he noticed that the clip board suggested he was a TV License Worker operating in the area. UUUM! That would be a bonus, then because we never had one of them for as far back as I could remember; as we walked on and never once looked back. Hopefully, the information regarding the resident "working abroad" may keep the wolf from the door.

Dad refused point blank to pay and resented the BBC and its politics, how they fed fake news. The only time he had ever been a part of anything to do with the station, was when he was locked up in Borstal as a young teenager. He had written to JIM WILL FIX IT, to see if Jimmy Saville would fix it for him to be released early. He had only done it as a joke and he doubted Borstal would have even posted the

227

letter. All of the other lads would have a laugh saying what if Dad walked out with a big badge on it saying "JIM FIXED IT FOR ME" L.O.L.

I would always need to act as a look out for Dad, as his eyes were now failing him more and more and he had already stated he would not be writing anymore books after he had given me help with this one. I had been to Birmingham to get them lasered, but they had been unable to do it, because of age and deterioration and I slowly became his eyes more and more. Having said that I would only assist him after I had, had my day's fun by letting him walk into a few walls or get on the wrong bus. He would need a white stick anytime soon, was my guess and although it was perhaps cruel it was far too comical to not let it happen. He had the occasional black eye; he hoped the neighbours didn't think he was suffering from domestic abuse, from me, as much as I'd like to give him the occasional slap or plank of wood round his head.

If his sight was in good shape he would have been able to see that his latest additions to the flat were a complete eyesore. Every bit of spare money he would be forever improving the flat and maybe he was striving to be a little more "middle class" like Hyacinth Bucket in THE GOOD LIFE /KEEPING UP APPEARANCES?? on TV.

He had only got four numbers on the lottery; anyone would have thought he had won a fortune. As he set about spending much more than he had won, as he splashed out on a mini "chandelier" and matching lamp with lots of fake glass baubles all dangling everywhere and is as garish an item as you would ever come across. "Looks nice don't it Stella"? He couldn't see me rolling about with my paws over my mouth, "it looks completely ridiculous" you very silly old man and he had excelled himself this time. Why anyone would ever want a fake chandelier in a council flat was beyond me but this is the sort of person I was living with. The worst thing was he would wish to have the light on all night so the baubles could reflect all around the room with its coloured light beams.

He had a habit of leaving lights on in every room. When he had spent all the time he did on security lists, in prison as a youngster, the lights in the cell would be left on all night; that was due to him being a security risk for escaping from previous prisons. They would probably enjoy disturbing his sleep, as many of them were sadistic like that. All it did, with this daft twat I live with, was sent him the other way and he leaves the lights on to sleep. None of that would ever inconvenience him, in the jail and he would sleep like a top, and it would be the exact same out here in our home.

The only thing that could ever disturb this man's sleep is yours truly because I would put my face perhaps an inch from his when I felt it was a "reasonable" time to get out of bed (usually seven am or even earlier L.O.L.). He would roll over to avoid my stare but after a quick had spring and a forward roll I would be in his face once again. Trust me once I started to become an annoying pest, the ONLY way to prevent that is to get out of that bed, get your clothes on and put that doggy bag in your back pocket because I am gagging for a number two. I called the shots in here, I'm the queen bee and the quicker he realised that the better. Anyway he should appreciate the early morning knock because it was much easier for me to come out of the shop with a jar of coffee in an early morning while everyone was half asleep. Out of all bad comes good!

CHAPTER TWENTY

His eyes might be getting bad but his fucking teeth weren't far behind him because every time I went to the bathroom, there would be more and more of them in a jar. They looked quite scary to me; I looked to make sure there wasn't another jar with his eyeballs in L.O.L. I bet the teeth wouldn't be in a jar if any girl was stopping the night though and in fact they could be cemented in with Fixodent on them occasions so he could perform satisfactorily.

I used to listen to him bragging to his friends that he was, in his words, the master of the mattress and apparently he had sparks coming off the sheets. He seemed to forget I was also in the flat and I didn't hear the earth move and I'm sure the girl upstairs never felt it move. I would watch the ladies leave on a morning and their faces didn't say "memorable" to me, while they called for a taxi so "Silly Bollox" stop keep thinking you are some sort of Casanova!

We needed to be up early today because a very young boy Owen Jones had been beaten up badly by three schoolboys' bullies and this had been very extreme. Owen had been left for dead on the riverbank and we needed to cheer him up. We got the family VIP tickets to go and see England play at Wembley, along with lots of other treats. Owen had a younger brother called Alfie, who had become very scared because of what had happened to his older brother. That's where I came in handy because I tap danced my way into the living room juggling tennis balls and all of the kids began to laugh. All kids love a little dog and I was no exception, as Dad and I took all of the kids down the canal and through the woods to the rope swings to give them all a little light relief.

Everyone and I mean everyone pulled as one to lift Owen's spirits, Charlie had sent Owen some unique art from his prison cell and Paula Salvador had got in touch to get Owen some new trainers. Our local Bikers chapter, also showed up to take the kids out on their Harleys and it was a beautiful little period for the children. For the life of me none of us can understand that level of violence, from young kids towards other kids, poor Owen's face was like a beach ball, brutalised so badly.

I used to love calling around for the kids and teaching them how to smile and laugh again but they have left the Estate because of the effect that it has had on them all. Why be that way kids and I always hear Dad telling you all to approach him if you ever feel bullied and he will go directly to see their parents and nip it all in the bud. Play nicely, no bullying and just grow up to be good friends and look after each other. All you Parents everywhere should tell your kids not to suffer in silence and tell somebody if you are being bullied. It is not acceptable.

We had heard a story about the local Ghurkhas pub, which was ran by our friend Carol Martin, it seemed it was being haunted by an old man and his Jack Russell. The joke around town was could everybody be sure that it wasn't just Dave Grinnell, coming back from the toilet with a white face because he'd had a lot to drink and it was me leading him back L.O.L. Joking aside though it was sounding like quite a few had seen the ghostly man and his dog and the story is well known to many. I thought it was quite funny and said to Dad, when we finally go can we come back and haunt Nuneaton Council in the Town Hall. God how I would love that! It would be hilarious, just making oooh and aaah howls and in a wailing voice keep repeating bedrooooom taxxx!   If one Jack Russell can haunt the town then I'm sure I can also do a good job. Not sure about "Silly Bollox" though he would struggle to spook himself to be honest.

He wished Carol well and set off into the town to have a few beers and me my customary swim in the fountain. Dad had a little bit of a dizzy spell and needed to sit down, his mate Mark from Birmingham who runs the flower stall by the fountain made him sit down and someone sent for an ambulance. Mark asked if I was going to be alright once the ambulance took Dad away, I would need to go up home because I had been given instructions, on what to bring to the hospital once it was dark and visiting time had finished.

It was very quiet later that night when I approached the George Eliot Hospital. I would be very difficult to spot along the white walled corridors because of me being so small and white myself. Dad had sent me a text message saying what Ward he was on, so I made my way up the stairs and slid into the Ward and under the bed where Dads arm was hanging over the side. Psst "I'm here" I whispered and a face popped over the side and I thought "oh fucking God, Dad looks really ill" and I feared the worst as I passed him the sachet of cocaine he had requested and I was really worried about him as I made my exit.

I hadn't been careful enough in my departure and a voice shouted "hey where have you come from"? Two Nurses were almost on top of me, they were that close I could even read their name badges, Lisa Bagshaw and Madeline Morris. A chase ensued where I kept ending up taking lots of wrong turns, I finally thought I was cornered and was up against the wall out of breath. When I was rescued by an apparent alarm having been rang on one of the Wards. It transpired that Dad had been moved to another Ward earlier, standard behaviour for any hospital really. The Patient; I had seen earlier had taken Dads place in that hospital bed; when I had squeezed the sachet in his hand and said "get that down you" he had done exactly that. He was now swinging from curtain to curtain like a rodeo star, he was doing that much screaming and he was slapping the Nurses arses and tearing at their clothes. All the other Patients cheered at the antics because it was always long boring days and this incident had definitely done a lot to change the atmosphere on the Ward. That was until Nurse Bagshaw, needed to take him out with a swift elbow chop to the throat and all the other Patients wolf whistled and cheered. Many of them had wet their beds with all of the excitement.

When I got home I had a text from Dad asking why I hadn't shown up at the Hospital. He told me of all the funny events in the Ward across from him and I thought it wise to not tell him I had visited the Hospital earlier.

Dad was released the following morning anyway and the relief I had of the realisation that was not him in the other bed was immeasurable. Whoever that was in that bed, he was certainly not long for this world and if I brought him a little light into his life last night then so be it. That would probably be the last time he ever swung on the curtains waving his dick in the air naked as a jay bird. Maybe it would be a good idea to throw a bag into each Ward at least once a week and at least let people die happily.

"Silly Bollox" was home with strict instructions to boost his diet and eat lots of steak; which was always likely to wind me up being as how my bowl was still only featuring celery or lettuce. If this fucking diet went on for too much longer I would do what all the local cats did and piss off out the door and go get fed at a different home. It's all well and good him fainting in the town but I was more than a little light headed lately and it was probably to do with my Atkins diet. Let's not worry about the Queen hey a long as the King s getting his T-bone steak and extras.

It was lucky he was forgetful because every time he went to the toilet or was distracted with his phone ringing, I was like a cheetah for a few morsels of meat from his plate. Well what would any of you do because just lately I may as well have been one of the IRA's hunger strikers; I was getting that little put out for me. The homeless were getting a sight more than me; Greggs must be cleaning up profit wise all of the food that gets bought for them.

On a serious note our town is now quickly catching other towns up, with the increase in people sleeping in doorways, which has increased tenfold. In particular with young teenagers, if you are unfortunate enough to find yourself between the ages of sixteen and twenty-five years old; than overnight your life, become a nightmare under the Tory policies. Our town is fortunate enough to have a charity headed by Carol Barnsley, which deals specifically with young teenagers but many other areas don't.

God Bless all you young homeless kids and Dad and I will always try to feed you no matter how skint we are because our situation could never begin to match your own. Don't expect things to change too much anytime soon, because nobody cares enough anymore about your situation except the aforementioned charity which you are lucky to have. There is even one young girl in a wheelchair and we walk by regular and see her asleep in the doorway of a disused shop; with her wheelchair folded up by her. If we see her then I'm quite sure people who work for the council also see her while they merrily walk to work in the Town Hall.

Does nobody at all have any shame anymore, that our Streets are full of homeless kids and veterans from our mis-guided war escapades? I'm ashamed to be part of any of it, but many of you simply choose to walk on by these people and give yourselves the easy option. I know many good people who work in that Town Hall, though many daren't speak out because everybody's job is under threat in the present climate and nobody is safe.

Central Government starve local Councils of financial support while they all eat lobster and quaff champagne in the comfort of Westminster. Whilst filling out bogus expense sheets and these are the sort of people who we are obliged to look up to; our very own pillars of society. They do not belong in our world and Dad always says if we have a roof over our heads and can afford our own little treats; then we were doing better than most.

As if to confirm that I was about to be booked in for a groom with Sal Stroud and Brad Webb; because I was the most famous dog in town I did not need to pay for my grooming. Instead I gave Shampooches Boutique, in Laburnum Grove, Camp Hill any publicity I could, which I did at every opportunity. It was like I did modelling work, I felt like the Kate Moss of Hill Top and I would swagger about like a model on the catwalk. I would always look my prettiest after I left their Parlour, Dad would never complain because Brad would always be making a breakfast while Sal tended to my needs. It was a very happy little arrangement and even transport was sent to pick us up and drop us back. Anything that helped us reduce our overheads was a Godsend in the present climate. When I walked out all groomed and smelling of scented perfume, I would look at Dad and Brad and indicate to them that it was that time again and they would all need to do their duty. All hail the Queen!

The only Nursing Home Dad and I used to pass seemed to have an ambulance outside every other week or a Funeral Directors car with the back doors open to discreetly place a body inside. It wasn't that unnoticeable to be honest and we would both look away out of politeness. It couldn't be much of a life just sat about waiting until it was your own turn to be slid into the waiting boot of a car. It would be much better to be clutching your heart with a losing hand of poker or a large line of cocaine whilst drinking your treble whiskey.

I knew Staff who worked at Nursing Homes now who wouldn't need much recruiting to come and work for me and my Dad; Catherine Fenton, Rachael Matthews, Alma Brookes and Lisa Bagshaw. They were all girls who could assist us in changing completely the hum drum routine of Care in the Community.

The Home would have its own resident tattooist to brighten up any tattoos that had dulled in colour down the years. It would be a win, win situation because with the swap around the Estate, some of the arseholes we witnessed being complete idiots, could be given Zopiclones to get them off to sleep and even the local Police would end up with many quiet nights and the ONLY possible place for there to be excess noise or any trouble would be the Nursing home.

The name of our Nursing Home would be Stella's Sinners. As the heroin addicts would be fast asleep due to the sleeping tablets, which would give our Residents free reign to help themselves. Should any of them fall behind with their rent, we would allow two or three to go out during the night with balaclavas and rob mountain bikes or whatever they could get their hands on. The Smack Rat Heroin Addicts would be crying and appealing on Social Media to get their things back, but all of the bikes would have been stripped down in the Workshop at the back of the Home. It would be impossible to recognise any of the bikes; the next time some of the other Residents would ride them about during the day to mug some of the other heroin addicts. It would be a complete reversal of what had been taking place in the past few decades, the previous lowlife thieves would be too embarrassed to ring Crime Stoppers, saying three female pensioners with studded leather jackets, had just robbed them of their dole money and they seemed drugged up.

They would all need to be home for their dinners though because dinner would be worth coming back for because it would not be anything like, all the disgusting Catering Companies, forty-three pence per meal situation that had been going on for years.

Young, old or disabled all seemed to be prime targets now to be taken advantage of and home some people slept was beyond me. How some people slept was an ironic statement, as our Residents would have no intention of sleeping, with memories of racing in fields still fresh in all of our minds and now we would all of us be double dropping our iron tablets. I'd imagine the Police would leave us undisturbed because crimes figures had gone down in the area.

I would be the Home's Resident Pet and wander from room to room getting fussed and in the unfortunate circumstance of anyone dying, at short notice. I could get my Rosary beads and Nun's outfit out and say a quick prayer at the side of the bed. Any Resident, being signed in by one of their children would not be lied to. They would be told that the life span of their parents would be dramatically reduced from the moment they set foot through the door but boy would they go out with a bang. There shouldn't be a problem and if anything the children's inheritance should now remain at a higher level with the seemingly quicker demise. They would be taught how to use a food processor to dilute cocaine powder, instead of blending food into soggy messes. Night classes would teach them how to spot heroin dealers and users so that we were sure they would be robbing the correct people.

At our Home they would be able to die with dignity instead of being bullied and ridiculed at many of the other Homes by the Staff or occasionally even by their own children. It's become a sad old world that many of us live in, much of what I write is aimed at being funny, throughout the book; but I am sure you have also noticed that I touch on a lot of very serious matters at the same time. Even with the funny stories, I have left it to your imagination which stories are true and which are fiction. I promise you this much and that is many of the tales you believe to be fiction are actually true and would shock you to your core.

Denzil Richards, the lad who lived next door said he would always look after Dad when he got older but in all honesty our own Nursing Home sounded much more fun. This generation of older people rocked more than any other and Dad and I were already aware of the Public House in Bedworth, JB's where all of the older drinkers with mobility scooters all sniffed cocaine.

It was the way of the world, even the toilets in the House of Commons, were infested with traces of cocaine all over the seats and it was now a lot clearer why they all talked all of the shit that they did. Jesus Christ! That could have been the perfect job for "Silly Bollix", to talk shit day in and day out because it was no more than what he did now. What had we all become hey, it may seem a little hypocritical for me to call them, while my Dad does what he does, BUT my Dad is not responsible for running a country is he and not answerable to anyone?

His life is his own and he is free to do with it what he wishes. He has lost many friends, much younger than himself, when they died and even his own Dad died at the age of forty. So his opinion was that life was to be lived and live every day like it is your last because one day it will be. He had no intention of ever dropping anchor or applying the brakes and felt no need to explain his actions to anyone. He did not wish to wear slippers or smoke a pipe, just yet and I doubt he ever would.

Even this last year which had been filled with much tragedy was a very harsh period. All we are left with is the option to march on because none of us can change a thing that has occurred. All we can do is look after each other as best we can and try and fill each day with laughter. Until hopefully one day that laughter outweighs the sadness.

I wish this daft twat, could have taken up politics though because he could have been the Dennis Skinner of Nuneaton and I could have chased that fucking cat all the way up Downing Street. It's always sat on the front step with a cosy little life, I would soon change that and I'm sure Dad would chase some of them spoilt little rich kids out of their comfort zones.

He has always been political and was a Shop Steward in British Steel for years and how he never got into the political side of it surprised me. I could just imagine the Speaker shouting ORDER! ORDER while Dad was stripping off in the middle of Question Time. With or without medication, he is more sensible than half of them in there.

We could have set about getting Independence for Nuneaton and build a bigger fountain but instead we are stuck with Marcus Jones M.P.; who votes to please his party instead of his constituents and I guess the ONLY time he visits Nuneaton is to pay a visit to Greggs. He seems to have led a charmed life does Marcus, as he was recently investigated for misuse of election funds. As is the case with all of these people the accusations were proved to be unfounded. Politicians' will always be a law unto themselves and never need to adhere to the restrictions imposed upon the rest of us.

I stopped treating any of it seriously when the M.P. used to hold his Surgery at MacDonald's in Nuneaton on a Saturday morning; for any of us to register complaints. So obviously the logic behind that was for us all to eat a Happy Meal while we registered any of our grievances' L.O.L. Either that or Gregg's was shut on the days he visited, but none of it mattered to me. While I would be jealous looking at the waistline of Marcus and everyone filling their faces with food; I was the little dog under your table with a stomach rumbling like an active volcano.

I suppose we had our calling in life and his had been into politics, whereas my path had taken in religion, where I would need to pray for the well being, of these people. Although, I wouldn't have thought that anyone earning in excess of £79,468 per annum, plus claiming every expense under the sun; certainly didn't need any prayers from me. Marcus would be no exception as he certainly didn't appear to be underfed as none of them do in Westminster, if you look closely.

Austerity, it seemed, only applied to certain sections of society and they weren't amongst the casualties; here on the other hand you had me the tiny Jack Russell that was getting more and more miniature by the day. AS I was suffering from Austerity and at the same time enduring the Atkins diet so I'm in double trouble.

Everybody keeps putting the fear of God into me, talking about food shortages after Brexit, trust me every time I pop my head around the door to check on that day's menu there seems to be already a shortage of food. Grrrr...Bastard!

I am giving the next chapter to my Dad who has a very important message to get across.

CHAPTER TWENTY-TWO

All I have to say regarding the recent death of Paula Salvador deserves saying and if I upset anyone I really don't care. This coming Monday, two days time, the funeral takes place of the wife of Charlie Bronson Salvador and some of you on-line need to hang your heads in shame the abuse you gave that young woman.

It was bullying of a very extreme nature and I attempted to defend her myself on many nights; but once I seen it was making no difference I told her to do the same as me and leave the Group. However, she chose not to, by now the bullies also had an audience which increased the abuse and much of it now also directed at Charlie who had no voice at all on your sites. I have never been in a rush to join other such like Groups since and even when people invite me I choose to ignore the requests and the ONLY sites I choose to be on are ran by gentlemen.

This one particular Group contributed to Paula's downfall because night after night, these people would not ease up until she was in tears. Of course she would give the impression that she was handling it and everything was fine but in private messages to me it was clear the abuse was taking its toll on her and why would it not?

She was very upset that she had even met one of the main culprits and he had been a friend but had now chosen to ridicule her. Others on your page even began to abuse Charlie and say he would ALWAYS stay in prison and didn't deserve to be out amongst us and when I spoke his corner I was told "well let him come live by you then because we don't want him living by us"!

Jesus Christ people! Who are you judgemental fuckers, hey, that can slate a man you have never met before. Yet give your opinions on his prison sentence and even wish him to spend more time in the jail. Forty-four years is obviously not enough punishment by your people's standards. Thank God none of you ever sit on any Parole Board that was connected to anyone in a prison, because they would not be coming home early would they?

Many of you are claiming Paula was just a gold digger were even selling Charlie's art on your site to make yourselves a quick shilling and I'm prepared to bet a million quid; that all of the juicy bits of gossip that the media got hold of, came from these same sources.

Some of you even had the nerve to be on pages, that were strictly for people who were interested in ACTUALLY getting Charlie out of prison but in my opinion you were there to see how it would profit YOU! My opinion for what it is worth is anyone who can wish a man to spend even one more night in any cell is never welcome in my company and never will be.

Then for the poor girl to be found dead and certain people still don't ease up and continue with loose comments, it's beyond belief. Paula never helped herself going amongst a pack of hyenas like Katie Price and Carol Maloney on Loose women. Like any of them are deemed to be experts in the relationship department or ever will be. They wasted no time in criticising Charlie and his situation although knowing nothing about him except for the media coverage, which gives a very twisted and biased opinion. Those people on that show were never going to be favourable towards Paula or Charlie. Whatever anybody's opinion of Paula was, the one thing none of you could disagree with, was she was tireless in her efforts to raise awareness for Charlie.

He has raised vast amounts for worthy charitable causes and in Nuneaton alone he helped at least a dozen different causes and people in need of assistance. Paula would be in touch with a little cancer girl Reagan, who had numerous operations. She has now rang the bell to indicate she has beaten the illness and her parents often thank Paula and Charlie. Another little cancer patient in Tamworth, unfortunately, was not so lucky and it hit Charlie bad at the time being as how the little boys name was also Charlie.

The help that gets given to other people and causes throughout the country, that gets no positive coverage from the Press. It saddens me and it did Paula, and she set about changing that pinion albeit at a great cost to herself; because the Press hounded and stalked her every move. It is the way our Press work and many before Paula have suffered the same consequences. What I can't understand is why; members of a criminally minded Group turn on people and post them up to be ridiculed.

Along the way while I have been on-line I have met many people, who are loyal and very genuine people and it has been a pleasure to meet these characters: Michael Nesbitt . Gary Dennis. Rod Harrison. Daz Holcroft. Ivor Batty..Tony Turner. Jason Sothers

There will be others I have overlooked, but I mention these names because I never hear any one of them have a bad word to say about anyone and they have obviously been brought up that way. Same as me they would glean no satisfaction whatsoever by bullying someone be it in real life or on-line and especially female.

It disgusted me reading a lot of the comments and once an insult raised a laugh then it encouraged others to come out of the woodwork and add their own insults to raise a few laughs with "the lads". This particular Group is always bragging about being the biggest in numbers. What you have to understand is that with that large roll call also becomes a much bigger audience and you are responsible for the material they hear. You have been able to see the consequences of your actions and I'd hope it prevented you doing the same again to anyone but somehow or other I doubt that.

It matters little to me that Paula had mental issues, because I myself have been treated under the Mental Health Act, since the mid 1970's because I admit I am a little mentally imbalanced but surely knowing of this would give you even less reason to brow beat a female to floods of tears every night. I am really at a loss to understand it all because it's all a little raw still and I certainly won't be attending the funeral because I wouldn't want to come across any fakes in attendance. God Bless Paula and her Family and I cannot begin to imagine their loss, maybe after Monday she can be left in peace and you trolls can go and find another victim.

All of you giving your opinions as to why Charlie WON'T get out make me laugh because it's all within touching distance now. It would probably help as well to achieve that, if one or two of you snakes stopped leaking rubbish stories to the Press to gain your thirty pieces of silver. As I say, I have met some perfect gentlemen but you other individuals who for some strange reason are just full of your own importance are never welcome in my company.

Each day I wake up I am happy to look in my mirror and see who looks back. I have never in my life, looked up to nobody but more importantly I have never look down on nobody either. I am now in my sixties, I am greeted warmly and with respect everywhere I go. If everybody conducted themselves in that fashion the world would be a better place, but unfortunately, there are others who prefer to bully cajole their way through life. I know which I prefer to be and although I'm not a complete saint, I am respected and approachable and that's good enough for me.

It shouldn't have to take the death of a young girl to question your behaviour but if it's touched even the slightest nerve with you then it has served some purpose. God Bless all you girls who had a protective arm around her at all times. You were a fun little crowd to watch from a distance but again your love for each other stretched beyond the wedding side of things because you were all complete friends and she would have been thankful to have you all: Beverleigh Zacher. Julie Preston. Paula Frankland. Diane Scriven. Linda Harrison

There are probably other's I've forgotten but you were all important to her and a big part of her life. She would have been very thankful to have you all around and I hope you all remain friends forever. It's an awful situation that we have all found ourselves in, the grief is real because we have lost a good friend between us but I am sure we can all keep her memory alive between us. I will never go on that Group again ever, out of respect to Paula and Charlie and if any of you ever see them people bullying people again then remind them of this period in time.

None of us can change the events that led up to all of this and all of the gossip and unfound allegations in the papers are uncalled for. That is the British Press I'm afraid, they print what they want. I'm sure that between us we can keep a much better memory of Paula alive hey! God Bless you all.

CHAPTER TWENTY-THREE

Back in the real world and due to Dads constant battle with the DWP, trying to get Personal Independent Payments (PIP), we were struggling again. Three years this had gone on now and we were still no closed to having the matter resolved.

I still pretended to everybody on the Estate that I was a Nun and it came in handy for the shoplifting, as I could secrete jars of coffee or the occasional tin of corned beef, After hiding it under my Nuns habit I would laugh that it was the ONLY beef got anywhere near my little mimmim.

Meanwhile, Dad had spotted an advert in the paper for volunteers at a big University, where the successful applicants would e fed drugs on behalf of one of the Pharmaceutical Companies that had only been tested on animals'. The pay was certainly good Dad had thought and he was also involved in his favourite past time which was consuming drugs. Oh dear! What could possibly go wrong, because if my memory served me correctly only recently about six different volunteers had been given a certain untried drug? They had all been placed in Intensive Care because they became very poorly and swelled up to the size of the Michelin Man in the tyre advert.

The money would be too good to refuse unfortunately, but it would always be a high risk venture and one that would always require a disclaimer to be signed before hand. He had been over to Loughborough to have his first session and when he came home. I had place two tins of corned beef on the coffee table and I thought he would be pleased but he seemed more interested in the contents of the fruit bowl and in particular the bananas. That was my day fucked up because I found it virtually impossible to open up the weird tins.

I looked over my shoulder and did I just imagine that or did he just run along the top of the settee and swing from one door handle to another? I took no notice, now he kept beating his chest while I tried to watch the TV; his behaviour was certainly a little strange. He seemed happy that we had a little money in the bank now, but I thought at what cost, as he again made a swinging action like a chimpanzee. "Fuck this" I thought I want my Dad back!

The risks some people take are not worth the effort to be honest. As they only monitor the short term effects of anything they have injected into anybody and would they really care if Dad was swinging from tree to tree in a years' time L.O.L. The symptoms only lasted for a day or so thankfully. What they didn't know about Dad was he would have needed a much higher dosage, as his tolerance to any drugs was way above any normal human being; I could vouch for that but even so I would prefer him not to use this route to acquire money anymore. It was far too risky and I worried for his health and sanity BUT I also worried more, who was going to open the fucking corned beef.

We would get Royalties from Amazon on the 29th of each month but nothing substantial. It was just a pittance really because it's a case of swimming amongst sharks because obviously the big multinational company take the bulk of the profit. We would need to sell a large amount of books, to be able to be a little comfortable and for that reason it's important to tell all of your friends about this book and previous ones we have written. It's either that or "Silly Bollox" will swing through the trees all the way back to get more injections. Knowing him and is curiosity about drugs, he would happily experiment without even wanting to be paid for any of the consumption.

I would need to stress to "Silly Bollox" the importance of not upsetting any of the Community Standards Police on Facebook; because he was banned every two minutes lately. It was no longer the seven day ban; it was not thirty days at a time. While the ban lasted it prevented Dad from working on his Author Pages and so prevented him from earning any book sales money which seemed a little but that was Facebook all over. It did not take much to receive a ban especially if you dared to be critical of the Israelis!

They should leave us both alone now as we were both getting old and had our share of health scares. Dad had stopped smoking almost a year now and seemed a little healthier and all we needed now was a little extra money. God knows how much I was owed in arrears for being his Carer; we could retire to the Bahamas. Never mind the Bahamas because right now even a long weekend in Yorkshire would satisfy me, especially now I spoke the local lingo. Hey up zitha, eeh bah gum; I could speak the tongue of the cobblestones easily now. You'd do well to see a hot tub up there, though you might get the tin bath filled with water from the boiling kettle. This was the land that time forgot BUT I loved it because I knew most of them were the exact same as my Dad, kind natured folk. Quick dip in the tin bath, then half an hour in the backdoor step with slices of cucumber on my eyes would be my idea of heaven. I wouldn't stay in the bath long because most Yorkshire men would throw their ferrets in for a soak. After a laze in the sun I would feel clean and on point but could do with a quick Brazilian to top it all off.

A male Jack Russell from up in Yorkshire was in touch on a regular basis and kept asking

272

when I was coming up? His name was Patch and I was sure I had an admirer. He thought I was Royalty and continually asked if I lived in a big country house because he couldn't understand why I had never hunted. He knew all of my history and was always calling me a Fallen Angel and he would have been surprised to know that I had even been to a Lap Dancing Club in Yarmouth with my Dad, called exactly that FALLEN ANGELS! It's not the customary behaviour to expect from your average Nun, but I was only there to keep my eyes on "Silly Bollox" because it doesn't take much of an excuse for him to strip off anyway and I would need to be on hand to prevent him getting beat up by the Bouncers. He would know the tell tale signs and if I began to "hump" his arms or legs then that would be the cue that it was time to go and bring him back to reality.

I had done it many times down the years. If I wanted unwelcome guests to leave, a few cheeky little "humps" and they would soon want to put their coats on. Some of the callers to the flat just weren't my cup of tea and especially when they would enquire "who lives here then? Just the two of you" because the only place that led was another waif and stray looking for accommodation and Dad didn't mind the odd night BUT no way did he want another passenger and apart from that where would all of "The Others" sleep. They would try to stop longer than the one night but would soon discover I was the Boss in here and they would be getting shown the door, straight after their Frosties in the morning. I had enough on my plate without there being another drugged up arsehole in the morning.

No way could I write a book while I had two people around me talking to themselves; I needed to focus since Dad had gone out of the game having not picked a pen up for a while and now it was left to me. I think Dad shocked

274

himself at how well his original books had done. The first two he had written because he had been expelled from both of his schools and dismissed as being not very bright and disruptive. He would be the first to agree about being disruptive because he certainly an agitating bastard and I could readily confirm that he was disruptive.

Even I would need a break from him some days and would just jump on a bus into town and have a stroll about or have a swim. Afterwards I'd go into my two favourite shops to see how the book sales were going, JOCO GIFTS in the Ropewalk Shopping Centre and Cooks Cakes opposite Iceland. Our books had been selling in the shops for four years and so I suppose it was safe to say that Dad had become an established Author now. He could be proud of that for years to come or his own children could be if he had not seen them by that time which seemed likely was going to be the case.

He had never hurt anybody and the children had been fed lies but he could do little or nothing about it, any of it. As is often the case with many men before, in similar circumstances, and many after the poison has already spread and nothing the Father says will change that opinion. The Father is a snake with seven heads apparently and is to be feared whereas all of this town will state differently, but far from the truth to get in the way of a good lie? We live our lives as best we can and ignore the abuse thrown our way.

I make Dad laugh and smile each day and we are much happier without any of the drama around us. Dad got away from a very, very strange family who have ruined other people's life's apart from his and even cost one poor man his life but we all need to look away, bury that and not speak ill of anyone. Disgraceful but Dad knows the truth and so do many others around here. Shame on them in the Family! The

Freaky Folans L.O.L.   Why don't they get themselves on Britain's got Talent, they would sail through the auditions.   It's a total embarrassment that Dad's Daughter walks around with the name Folan, when it's not even that Family's name. You couldn't make it up and it needs saying because he won't ever get a chance to say it face to face.

There's much more to it, but in a book is not the right place, to shame them all and we would rather have no contact at all with any of them. People walking around with names that are not even their own, very strange carry on. I have spoken to the mother of the poor man who died and she is far from happy that his surname has been stolen. What a carry on and now the next generation is stuck with the pretence and his Daughter, Demi is stuck with the surname. Anyway it is in print now but to be honest most of Nuneaton knows the lie. Enjoy your day!

You will never disturb our lives and we are far happier than you lot and we have no guilt to deal with. Come and have a tap dance on the coffee table with me L.O.L. I will say a prayer for you, but for now I have wasted enough time on you all.

CHAPTER TWENTY-FOUR

Right then as we near the end you all have to decide when Dads writing or when I am writing or maybe even some of "The Others" while we are asleep.

Dads already planning ahead for success with this book and he had just taken me for a full groom to sharpen me up ready for the book launch. He calls me the "Kate Moss of Hilltop" and I must admit I do know how to shake my booty when I'm feeling all freshly groomed. "Silly Bollox" always takes things a little too far though and after watching him conduct some shady business in the corner of a pub. When he came back he showed me a pretty collar that was adorned with brightly coloured glass, which even the most stupid person on the planet, would know that it was glass, but Dad once again out done himself by buying a "diamond" dog collar for me. I shook my head in disbelief and I dare not ask how much he paid but his heart was in the right place, I suppose because he always put me first and always wanted the best for me.

Once we got home he went upstairs with a metal box he had also bought and after what seemed an eternity of him banging with his hammer he came down to declare we now had a Sunken Safe in the bedroom floor and when I took my collar off on an evening I was supposed to place it in the Safe! Now I definitely didn't dare ask how much he had paid! He gathered a few items together what he deemed to be valuable and it must have resembled a Magpie's nest, as he placed anything shiny in the Sunken Safe. As if he still didn't feel happy he took his wallet out of his pocket, empty I might add, and placed that in there as well. I was laughing hysterically, when he had taken my collar off and placed a cheaper dog collar around my neck; and the contents of the Safe wouldn't even buy a burglar a bag of chips to be honest.

Oh he was a funny man to live with and the craziest thing was the EVERY single visitor we had, he would say to them that we had a Sunken Safe now and then proceed to show them, exactly where it was L.O.L. I thought the whole purpose was to conceal your valuables but this daft twat would tell everyone. It was lucky we weren't wealthy because everyone on the Estate would know where we kept our possessions, including the local shopkeeper and even the bus driver. If ever he went out and left me on the rare occasion alone. I would set up loads of traps because I imagined being home alone and every burglar in the town making for our flat.

It was lovely life though, all in all, because would anyone rather have a life of boredom because I certainly wouldn't. My life span is shorter than any of you and I would fill my days with laughter and wouldn't swap it for the world. He was definitely mad and a complete nutcase but I would laugh at all of his activities BUT always stop him just short of the people in the white coats turning up.

On the few occasions when he writes in this book, I am quite sure you can all see for yourselves how the mood alters in the writing. This is because he is never the same person two days running, but if anything that's what makes it more exceptional each time that he completes a book or helps me to write one. It is not an easy task and neither of us ever read anything back; so things may even get repeated occasionally and we would both apologise in advance for that.

We would never let fame change us and this is the fifth book we have written now and if we had any intention of moving to Beverley Hills we would have done it already. My only intention is to make people laugh and Dad has had many messages from lonely people saying that they love reading about my adventures on Social Media. It's perhaps the only laugh or smile they get and Dad has made it clear to them all, that they should not feel lonely and that I belonged to EVERYBODY and everyone of you was my wider family now and there was no need at all to feel isolated. He wished he could bring me to meet every one of you in person and especially if any of you were ill and housebound. He is right and I will tell you this that every time I wag my tail, it wags, for every one of you.

My main task in life though would be to keep "Silly Bollox" out of a strait jacket. He had taken a few bad turns in life but hopefully that was now behind him and he behaved himself now; if you excused the odd bout of nudity or him roaming about with a machete like the Texas Chain Saw Massacre.

He had been to prison on a few occasions which was sad really because you all know who have met him that he is a genuine soft hearted person. In actual fact the last three years imprisonment that he served, he was owed seven thousand pounds. When he went in and that was for giving people drugs on credit which they never paid and so in effect he was that kind that he was walking around an exercise yard for doing no more than GIVING drugs away for FREE. Sounds about right if you know this daft twat but I would rather have someone with a giving nature than the greedy grasping sorts.

We were inseparable and the whole town knows us, we could be found on the back seat of many buses and waving to everybody like Royalty each now day. We took it a stage further and were informed of a barge trip that took place regularly.

Dad and his friend Glen Pardoe showed up for the barge trip with crates of beer and a bottle of vodka, as if it was a booze cruise similar to the ones abroad. They had been misinformed and while all the other "shipmates" sat drinking tea and listening to Cliff Richard and Gerry and the Pacemakers; Dad and Glenn proceeded to empty the crates of beer. It was a funny day out once them pair began dancing about on deck. A meal had been arranged at one of the pubs but it would have been a good idea to carry on past until they had found a spot to turn the barge around BEFORE we went to the pub to eat and drink. Everything is conducted in a serious manner and then once we had left the pub the "Captain" of the ship seemed a little unsteady on his feet and that was quickly confirmed when he got stuck trying to turn the barge around with a punt. By now the wind had blown his Captains hat off his head all while Cliff Richards was belting out; "We are all going on a Summer Holiday". Dad and Glenn were by now swigging freely from the vodka bottle. Even Jack Nicholson in One Flew Over the Cuckoo's Nest, couldn't sort this situation out.

As you all know, it can take an eternity to cover even a few miles at a snail's pace on a barge and by the time I scampered down the gang plank, my ribs were aching with laughter. "LAND AHOY" Dad shouted to the Captains Bridge but he didn't appear to be happy but maybe that was because he had lost his Captains hat. To others that may not seem much of a day out, but the point of it is Dad would always fill my days with adventure and that should be the case with every pet owner. I was sure I gave Dad as much laughter as he did me! He ran me a bath and then I slipped into my Scooby Doo dressing gown and pyjama and we both had a cosy night and we had a laugh about yet another eventful day and the Captain having too much rum L.O.L.

How many adventures can a little dog expect to have in a lifetime? I would never be left alone indoors looking out of a window all bored. My life would never be that way and another incident with a Captain and his boat came about in Yarmouth with the Coast guard Crew.

As always I dived headlong into the sea on the beach, while waves crashed in and out; but due to my size, I had been carried out a little more and a little more; until Dad thought I was waving but the reality was I was having difficulties. The Life Guard on his high chair had spotted this and as is customary notified the Boat Rescue but also he would attempt to swim to me. Although, by now I had latched on to a loose piece of wood floating on the water; as the Coast Guard swarm past me. I rode a large wave like Bart Simpson on his skateboard, with my arms out for balance and just used the wood as a surf board. So okay I lied! It didn't really happen like that BUT I did have to grab some wood and a

Life Guard did swim out to rescue me, as the waves carried me further out with each wave. It was a scary moment and Dad finds me big streams on the beach now rather than the sea itself. I ran along the beach like Pamela Anderson in Baywatch, the only difference was how flat chested I was.

I was a lucky girl that day and ass a show of gratitude I spent most of the day picking up discarded rubbish left behind by you selfish people and again I felt lucky that none of your plastic had wrapped around me while attempted to swim to shore. Have a good look at yourselves and correct your behaviour, there is no need to be that way. Had it not been for you lot though I'd have not got a chance to meet the Life Guard who was quite hot and muscular; the two things "Silly Bollox" was not.

I had always kept our canals clean at home and could always be seen coming out and depositing empty pop bottles on the side. The only time that backfired and I never had the lead on I was in the middle of the canal and tugging and tugging; attempting to drag a supermarket trolley out of the water. I could hear Dad uttering "for fucks sake we will be here all day now" because he knows I am not a defeatist. Our canals are the same as our seas and why you all think it's justified is beyond me.

I have not been to the seaside for a while now and the whole purpose of this book is to raise money towards a Bikini Break for me. The more sales there are it will be greatly appreciated as I need some sun and sand on my cute little ass girls! I need your help to get there and definitely have another peep at the Adonis in the high chair. I have taught myself to surf since but I am quite sure I will still need rescuing L.O.L. So my fate is in your hands people, let's get me on holiday for all of the laughs I have given you throughout the year.

Thank you I love you all xx

Can you all tell "Silly Bollox" that I am the breadwinner now and there are to be no more doggy diets for the foreseeable future?

CHAPTER TWENTY-FIVE

Obviously, this book is written very much tongue in cheek and you all either get our sense of humour or you don't I'm sure many of you who follow me and Stella on Social Media will get the humour for sure and that's all we set out to do.

If we can raise even one smile between you then our work is complete and it gives us a great deal of satisfaction. All of us go through so much sadness lately and any relief from that is very much welcomed, I'm sure.

All of you are aware already of how cute a dog I am but to confirm it for you I will be enclosing lots of photographs here for you to witness, just how beautiful I am and my next career choice is likely to be modelling, once my name becomes a Brand Name.

So you must all remember the name STELLA G. GINNELLY, as you will soon be seeing me on all of the billboards. Right then my paw is dropping off with all this writing, so I wish all of you best wishes and if I make you laugh then I am pleased.

As I said we never read back, so we have to hope for the best and that we have been more funny than serious because that was the original plan.

All in all I would never swap one minute of my life. When you live with a schizophrenic it is like waking up to a different owner every day and you never know what is coming next and nothing is organised and I find it a perfect way to live.

Dad always got me to school and made sure I had the best of everything and he always schooled me in the ways of life and always involved me in everything and I grew with the exact same political views as him which always appeared to be on the side of the underdog and rightfully so. I was a slow learner and did not do very well at school but all of the teachers liked me and always spoke when they seen me on the estate or around the local town. I left with no qualifications as such and I had to settle for menial work and one of my jobs was cleaning at my previous school. At least I was paying my way because prior to that Universal Credit were only paying me £3 PER MONTH and most days we were eating grass, like a cow, for our lunch lol.

Once I got the job we bought a larger coffee table to celebrate and we BOTH got on top of it together and done a tap dancing duet whilst high fiving each other dancing to our favourite songs and the way things were looking we would need to buy an even larger one on the off chance our friend Charlie finally got an early release from prison and all the three of us could tap dance through the night. I would also need to teach Charlies dog a few steps. I had recently met him and it was hilarious how they say a dog looks like its owner because CHAS looked just like his with his own special brand of moustache. We are all rooting for his release and the day it comes he can tap dance his way out of the gate singing his version of Frank Sinatra My Way because after 43 YEARS he would have certainly done it HIS WAY. I lead a very full life and all of us dogs are only here for a short period but I will tell you this for free I feel as if I have been here forever and I have laughed and laughed until my ribs ached our lives are that chaotic and I would rather it be that way than lead a peaceful humdrum existence.

I had a harsh beginning but all of that was worthwhile now to have had the opportunity to meet and live with "silly bollox". I have been around the country and met many good friends, visited Buckingham Palace, handed a petition to

Downing Street and chased their cat. There is no other dog that leads a fuller life than me and dad and I are both going to grow old together and I doubt very much we will be doing it gracefully.

I went to watch The Stone Roses at Heaton Park in Manchester when they reformed and I quickly realised I was not cut out to be a nun after all and, if anything, you lot need to pray for me.   I am hoping you have enjoyed my adventures because the onset of cataracts means that this will likely be my last book.

We are both practically retired now and the love me and this daft twat have for each other is a very special bond. Romeo and Juliet. Anthony and Cleopatra and Stella G and "silly bollox" must all be mentioned in the same breath when talking of historical partnerships.

Our books will live on long after we have both gone and I shall be donating more copies to the local library and it has been a pleasure to even bring one smile to a sad face. Dad said I belong to you all and that is very much correct. I am

YOUR little dog and I am happy to bring a little sunshine into your lives. If anyone feels a little down then go and read my silly stories and cheer yourself up. I don't have many dull moments living with this one and so I have my share of laughter. He is stood in the window now waving to everyone on the hill again BUT he has forgot to get dressed again. Standard behaviour now to be honest. I doubt I would recognise him with his clothes on lol. Its time to go people but not before I say God bless you all and I feel such a special little dog to have all of the love shown to me by every single one of you. It's a two way deal because while I get shown the love I will look after "silly bollox" in return. "Au Revoir Shipmates". Yes, by the way, I was taught French at School .

Stella when she was a pup

WELLIES & WARDERS

A true tale of one man's struggle to overcome the harsh
realities of life, Borstals and the Prison System.

By Dave Ginnelly

My beautiful daughter Demi

Me and my pal Raff

Rest in Peace, my nephew Bradd

Bradd, Dale, my son David, me, my brother Glenn

Rest in Peace Darren Carter AKA Kenny Kitbag

Me and Frosty at Kenny Kitbag's funeral

Stella's hot tub

Stella's pal Diva

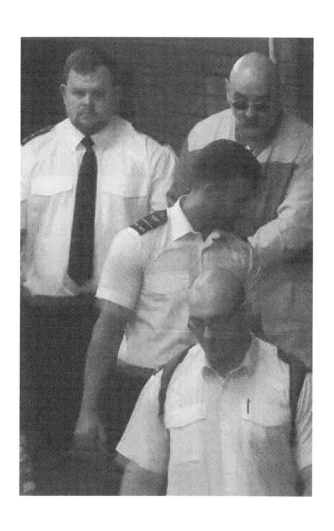

4 books by me
Dave Ginnelly
can be bought on
amazon
or via myself
with payment up front.
I may also sign it for you
winner winner..

Me and Dad with little Bella Timson

Stella's groomer's

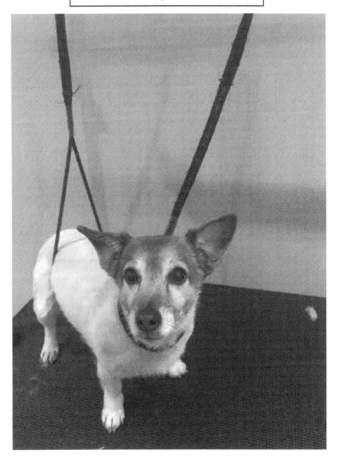

My great nephew Rohan

Me, Paula and Matt

Stella waiting for a photo finish

326

329

330

Rest in Peace Paula

Bradd's funeral, me, Lee, Joe and Trev

Me and Amarii

Me in Manchester, Stone Roses

Charlie's dog Chas

Off to see
Charlie with dad

Charlie's petition,

Downing Street

Me and my son Troy

Its a
Dogs Life

Dave Ginnelly

Printed in Great Britain
by Amazon